THE HOLLYWOOD **BOOK TWENTY-TWO** MURDER MYSTERIES

1968

THE MAN
IN THE
RAINCOAT

PETER S. FISCHER

www.petersfischer.com

The Man in the Raincoat

ISBN 978-0-9960491-9-1

To my bright and beautiful daughter
Megan,
now and always,
an indispensable part of my life.

PROLOGUE

Just when I thought that Nate Haller had once again slipped away undetected, I spotted him in line at the bank waiting for the next available teller. It was Friday, the 19th of April and the weekend was at hand. I guess Haller had run out of cash and for a man who pays in greenbacks for the tawdry little secrets of the rich and famous, an empty wallet is even worse than an unwinnable law suit. I'd been told he'd been spotted at the commissary but when I showed up, out of breath from having jogged all the way from Frankenstein square on Universal's back lot, he was gone. Jennie Frobisher, the sharp babe in charge of seating in the executive dining room, told me Haller had just left and was headed for the Black Tower on the other side of the plaza.

The Black Tower is an ebony edifice situated next to the main gate at Universal Studios. It houses the lawyers, CPA's and programming executives that make up the business arm of MCA, Universal's parent company, and its fourteen stories dwarf any other building located within the limits of Universal City, California. The building is utilitarian but it also sends a message from Jules Stein, the powerful head of the Music Corporation of America which has just absorbed Universal for a substantial amount of money. We are in the movie business, the Tower shrieks, and we are in the business to stay. Dismiss us at your own peril. Stein, along with his number two, Lew Wasserman, is the chief 'suit' in a tribe of hundreds of interchangeable 'suits' who toil tirelessly and ceaselessly to elevate Universal from second rate status in the Hollywood hierarchy to a position equal to MGM and the other prestige studios. Few doubt Stein's ability to succeed. Small in stature, he is a giant in the entertainment world and his eye for talent is legendary. So, too, some say, is his association with powerful elements of impolite society who keep batteries of lawyers working around the clock to ensure that day to day business continues uninterrupted by overzealous governmental entities. Or so it is rumored.

Every floor of the Tower is devoted to MCA-Universal save one, the main floor lobby, which has been leased to the Bank of America. Located here are the elevators and staircases that lead to the rest of the building. As I said, tipped off by Jennie Frobisher, I had hurried to the Tower. The first thing I saw was Bart Kane standing near a bench smoking a cigarette. Sitting on the bench was Gladys Primm, Haller's private secretary. I know one thing: where there is Bart Kane, Nate Haller is close at hand. Sure enough, as soon as I entered the bank, I spotted Haller on the teller line. I also spied Greg Lunsford at one of the counters filling out a deposit slip. Greg, garbed spiffily in his usual three-piece grey flannel suit and crimson power tie, had looked from me to Haller and back again, an expression of alarm crossing his face. He had been among those present the day before when, for the second time in three days, I had threatened Haller's miserable life. Perhaps Greg suspected the worst was about to take place. I have a thick skin when it comes to threats and barbs directed at me but when my beloved wife, Bunny, is made the target of scurrilous attacks by the likes of Nate Haller and his miserable rag of a magazine, the rules of civilized conduct no longer apply.

I had started toward Haller, murder in my heart, but at that moment, he'd spotted me approaching and quickly ducked out of line, hurrying for the nearby door that opens onto the stairwell. I charged after him but as I did, an elderly woman stepped in front of me and I bowled her over. She cried out. I, too, fell to the ground, banging my knee, as I heard a nearby woman scream. A man shouted at me loudly. Patrons scurried every which way to get out of the way as I struggled to get up. Out of the corner of my eye I saw Rico, the security guard, pull his weapon, not sure of what was happening. Suddenly an alarm sounded and I knew what that meant. Lockdown. Some befuddled teller had assumed a robbery might be in progress and had pushed the panic button. I should have stopped and let Haller go but something told me to stay on his tail. He'd eluded me twice today. He wasn't going to do it again. I limped to the stairwell door, flung it open and started to climb the stairs, my knee aching with every step. Above me I could hear the clattering of Haller's feet echoing in the stairwell. I wasn't far behind him but I was losing ground.

It hit me on the tenth floor landing. I was already gasping for air and my legs felt like oak logs, still I kept going. Haller remained above me, moving more slowly, more quietly. Suddenly a stitch in my side doubled me over in pain and I could only thank God it wasn't my heart. I staggered to the door that accessed the tenth floor and threw it open. An office was opposite, its door ajar. A secretary was working at her typewriter.

"Did a man just come through this door?" I gasped.

She looked up, uncomprehending.

"What?"

I repeated myself loudly, obviously annoyed. She shook her head. I ducked back into the stairwell unsure. Either way I had to continue. I struggled to the eleventh floor and repeated the process, opening the door to the corridor. The kid from the mail room was a few doors down at his cart sorting letters. I hurried to him wincing and repeating my question. No, he said, no one had come through the door. I turned and headed back to the staircase. Once on the landing, I looked up. Three more floors to the roof. I saw a shaft of light, then a resumption of darkness as a door above me slammed. Haller had reached the roof. I quickened my pace as best I could, stumbling past twelve and then fourteen which housed the executive offices occupied by Lew Wasserman and Dr. Stein. He wouldn't have ducked in there. Nobody ducks in there without an appointment, not even God.

Totally winded I reached the door which accessed the roof and pushed. It flew open propelled by a gust of wind and slammed against a wall. My eyes scanned quickly for some sign of Haller. He was nowhere in sight but I heard loud and excited voices coming from below. I also heard the whine of police cars approaching the scene. The LAPD division in Van Nuys had received the lockdown silent alarm and squad cars had been dispatched. So had a helicopter. I could barely hear the whirr of it's blades but I spotted it approaching at rooftop level from the west.

Curious about the commotion below, I held my aching side and hobbled over to the edge of the roof and looked down. A crowd had gathered and it was easy to see why. A body was splayed on the entrance road next to the security shack. There was no question of his identity. Light colored sports jacket, navy blue slacks. It was Nate Haller. I could see two officers from Jake McElrath's security detail racing up the street toward the scene. As I peered down suddenly someone spotted me and pointed skyward. Others followed suit. Some asshole with a camera took my picture. I started to back away, then realized that the chopper was swooping toward me. A voice shouted at me through a bullhorn.

"Raise your hands and drop to your knees! This is the Los Angeles Police Department. Do as you have been instructed. Raise your hands and drop to your knees!"

A uniformed cop holding a riot gun was hanging unsteadily onto the chopper frame, half in and half out of the cab, staring me in the face. Instantly I realized my predicament and self-preservation grabbed me by the throat. Run like hell! Get off the roof! Now! I turned and ran toward the doorway which had been wide open but now was closing. I thought I glimpsed a flash of grey flannel and then it was gone as the door slammed shut. I was a few yards from the door when I heard shots and the door was peppered with bullets. I looked back at the chopper.

"On the roof! Do not move. Raise your hands and drop to your knees!"

Not me, pal, I thought, as I took three loping strides to the door, pulled it open, and ducked inside. A hail of bullets clunked harmlessly off the now closed steel door. The staircase landing was dim. The single light bulb above the doorway provided little illumination. I moved toward the staircase and stumbled, falling forward, banging my knee again. It hurt like hell. Momentarily unable to stand I edged toward a nearby wall. My body was shaking, not from the chill of the stairwell, but from fear. I could hear footsteps on the stairway below. Someone was hurrying downward. The grey flannel was not imaginary but even a fool could recognize the situation I was in and I am no fool. At that moment I was quarry and it was just a matter of time before I was run to ground.

The sound of the chopper's rotors was louder than ever but steadier once the shooting had stopped. I scrabbled back to the door and opened it a crack, peering out. The chopper was motionless atop the roof, engine at full throttle. The pilot was on the roof, bending over the shooter who was grasping one leg, his face grimacing in pain, having obviously slipped from his perch. A slightly built female, the pilot, was trying to help the burly shooter back onto the chopper but it was no use. Words were exchanged. The pilot nodded and helped the shooter settle back onto the roof, then hopped into the cab and operated the controls. The chopper lifted off and then swooped away, undoubtedly in search of a medic and perhaps a new shooter as well. In fact, maybe more than one. To them I was unfinished business. I ducked back into the stairwell. Time to get a move on.

I thought to myself, how in God's name did I get myself into this situation? Four days ago all was right with my world. It was late Monday afternoon. I was home, puttering about, looking forward to a warm and inviting dinner with the girls as well as a good friend and one of my favorite people. How could my well-ordered life have turned to crap so quickly? I can't shut the past four days out of my mind. The events are sharply etched in my brain.

CHAPTER ONE

Call him the man who came to dinner. My daughter Yvette calls him the funny man after his performance in 'The Great Race'. Pretty soon I'm going to be calling him the man in the raincoat.

Only rarely do Bunny and I have someone over for dinner. When we entertain friends we usually hit a favored restaurant and pick up the tab. Don't ask why that is, we've always been like that, something about keeping our home separate and private from co-workers and even friends, a retreat reserved for us and Yvette and our beloved housekeeper/nanny, Bridget O'Shaugnessy. Tonight's Sunday evening dinner is an exception. Tonight we play host to Peter and Alyce Falk, relative newcomers to southern California. Peter is also a relatively new client of Bowles & Bernardi, the management firm which bears my name and to which I still am attached if only tenuously. These days I mostly write novels for a living. In the case of Peter Falk I have willingly jumped back into the management fray, at least temporarily.

My relationship with Peter blossomed shortly after he received his second Oscar nomination for 'Pocketful of Miracles'. He decided he wanted to become a permanent part of the Hollywood movie scene and my partner Bertha and I were only too happy to accommodate him. He turned out to be a dream client who needed no selling. Everybody wanted a piece of Peter Falk and for the past several years he has been going from one top movie to another, always in a juicy supporting role and always garnering terrific reviews: *Robin and the 7 Hoods, The Great Race, Luv, It's a Mad, Mad, Mad, Mad World*. He keeps working and keeps amassing more and more new fans. And now tonight, we are going to have a celebratory dinner to kick off a new opportunity in his fledgling career, a movie in which Peter, for the first time, is the acknowledged name above the title star. Granted, it is hardly 'Citizen Kane' and it is not a theatrical feature but a television film; however it is a terrifically plotted cop show with great dialogue, first rate twists and turns and a lead character, a detective lieutenant named Columbo, that any actor would sell his first born to play.

I'm in the living room opening a bottle of cabernet sauvignon to give it time to breathe before serving it with dinner. Knowing Peter as I do, we're having New York steaks, fries and asparagus with a green salad on the side and a chocolate seven-layer cake for dessert. Peter is a man of plebian tastes who enjoys good food but to the best of my knowledge that enjoyment does not extend to mussels, tofu, hummus, brussel sprouts, truffles or sweetbreads or anything else you can't order at the Carnegie Deli in New York City.

The doorbell chimes. He's here. I head for the front door. Yvette is at a friends doing homework and expected home momentarily. As I said, at 13, she is one of Falk's youngest fans off of his marvelous performance in 'The Great Race' with Tony Curtis and Jack Lemmon. She has no idea Peter has been invited to dinner. I can't wait to see her face. As for Bunny, she is in the kitchen helping Bridget. Bunny is also a huge fan and has been for years.

"Company!" I shout as I pull open the front door. Peter's standing there, a grin on his face, a sight to behold. He's wearing a weather beaten old raincoat over a rumpled brown suit and a polka-dot tie, and he has an unlit, half-smoked cigar jutting from his teeth.

He spreads his arms proudly.

"Well, whatdaya think?" he asks.

"About what?" I ask back.

"My get-up. My wardrobe," he says.

I cock my head appraisingly.

"I think you've been shopping at the Salvation Army again," I say.

"What? No. You mean the raincoat? This is my coat, Joe, i've had it for years. I just found it hanging in the closet last week. Nice huh?"

"Terrific," I say.

When I first met Peter Falk he was rummaging through old over-coats at a Salvation Army outlet in New York, looking for just the right one to wear for his role as Abe Reles in the movie 'Murder Inc.' It isn't that Peter dislikes wardrobe people, he just doesn't trust them to dress him properly for the roles he plays and more often than not his instincts are better than theirs.

I am dubious. "This is what the well-dressed LAPD homicide detective is wearing these days?" I ask.

"Who said anything about well-dressed?" Peter replies. "Chaplin had his derby hat and a cane. I got this. You mind if I come in? Thanks very much."

He breezes past me into the foyer. Before I close the door I get a good look at his car parked at curbside, a beat-up grey convert-ible of dubious parentage in bad need of a paint job.

"Nice car, Pete," I say as I close the door.

"A real honey," he says. "I found it on Universal's transportation lot this morning. The guys tuned it up and said I could drive it it tonight just to try it out, see how I liked it. I gotta drive it tomorrow afternoon over by the Beverly Hills Police Department."

"I get it," I say. "Columbo's car."

"Of course Columbo's car," he replies indignantly. "You think I'd be caught driving that thing around my neighborhood?" He looks around appraisingly. "Hey, Joe, this is some house you got

here. Really terrific. Should I have wiped my feet or something?"
He lifts his foot to see if any repulsive matter has accompanied him
to my front door. It hasn't.

Before I can answer, Bunny appears, hurrying toward us, smiling in welcome. A hug and an air kiss.

"Mr. Falk, I am so delighted you could come. It's wonderful to
meet you at last."

"Hey, none of that Mr. Falk stuff. I'm Peter. You're—uh—Wait.
Don't tell me."

"Bunny."

"Right, Bunny. And he's Joe."

"I know," she smiles. "I'm married to him. And where's your
wife? I thought she was coming."

"Yeah, so did I but Alyce got stuck in New York. You know how
these women are? Bridal party for this one, baby shower for that
one. My wife she's got girlfriends she hasn't even met yet. Yesterday
her best friend, Sylvia Bloom, and believe me, they're all her best
friends, Sylvia's having a divorce party and I ask Alyce, a divorce
party, what kind of thing is that, and she says they're celebrating
because the papers came through and I'm thinking this is a real lousy
thing, a bunch of gals sitting around celebrating Hyman Bloom's
pocket being picked for half of everything he's got. Is it right? I
don't think so but maybe that's just me."

All the while he's talking I'm helping him out of his raincoat
which I hang on the coat tree by the front door and we walk into
the living room. He suddenly becomes aware of the dead cigar in
his mouth and he removes it, fiddles for a moment and then starts
to put it in his shirt pocket.

"I'll take that, Pete," I say reaching for it.

"No, that's okay. I'll finish it later," he replies. "A quarter each,
I don't want it to go to waste."

Just then the front floor opens and Yvette bounds in, heading for the staircase. Having recently entered her teen years, her bean-pole frame is starting to show the first signs of womanhood but she has yet to acquire the all-knowing pseudo sophistication of a teenager and she takes on life with all the joyful abandon of an innocent ten-year-old.

"Yvette!" I call out. "Come on in. There's someone I want you to meet."

She stops short at the landing and starts in, just as Peter turns to face her with a warm smile.

"How ya doin', Yvette?" he says, getting to his feet. "Nice to meet you."

My daughter stops short, her jaw drops to her midriff and she regards our visitor in stunned silence. Then she turns, races from the room and mounts the stairs, two steps at a time. Peter looks at me helplessly.

"Was it something I said?"

"It isn't often she comes face to face with one of her idols. She'll get over it."

"I certainly hope so," Peter says. "I'm not used to frightening little children."

I was right. She does get over it and by the time we're busy eating, Yvette has turned into a little chatterbox and Peter is regaling us with stories of his school years in Ossining, New York, in the shadow of Sing Sing prison where he was the only kid in school with both a glass eye and a wicked sense of humor.

"So this umpire calls strike three on me on a ball so far outside I couldn't reach it with a fishing pole. I turn around and tell him what I think of his skills and he tells me to shut up and go sit on the bench which is when I pop out my glass eye and offer it to him because it's obvious he needs it a lot more than I do."

Bunny and I laugh and Yvette shrieks with delight and Peter laughs along with her. It's a dinner my little girl will not soon forget.

A few minutes later us grownups take coffee and cake out onto the patio while Yvette races up the stairs to call her closest friends to tell them all about her movie star dinner. It's while sitting outside in the cool evening air that Peter lifts the mask a little. He has re-lit the stub of a cigar he had stashed in his shirt pocket and Bunny has asked him why he's decided to do television when he has a successful movie career going. Is it the role?

"Yeah, that's a big part of it. The other part is, I'm tired of being the third guy through the door."

Bunny looks blank and glances over at me for help. Peter explains.

"Here's how it works, Bunny. The bad guy bursts into the room. His henchman, his number two, is right behind him. Then comes the third guy. That's me. I get a decent role and a nice paycheck but basically, I'm nobody. Now with apologies to Mr. Brando, I intend to be somebody but it hasn't happened. I'm in a rut and going nowhere which is where Joe and Bertha come in and they have found this great script with a great part and I don't care if it's being shot in an igloo in the ass-end of Alaska, this is what I am looking for so tomorrow morning I'm gonna show up on Stage 12 in my suit and my raincoat and take steps to broaden my career. End of story."

And he's right. That's the end of the story but he has omitted the journey that got him to this point. Lt. Columbo started off as a character in a short story written by Richard Levinson and William Link who then converted it into a stage play entitled 'Prescription:Murder' which was produced in San Francisco starring Thomas Mitchell. Jump forward to last year when it was again rewritten, this time as a two hour television movie which was snapped up by NBC. As envisioned by Levinson and Link, Columbo was a shuffling, seemingly absentminded bear of a man well into his fifties. The part was offered to Bing Crosby who politely declined since It would interfere with his golf. Lee J. Cobb was approached. Not interested. Several others were considered. Peter wasn't even on the radar screen but I was sure he'd be terrific so I talked the director, Dick Irving, into looking at some film on Peter. Dick already knew Peter's work but a second look convinced him. He agreed with me. Peter wasn't Levinson and Link's idea of Columbo but he had the tools and personality to pull it off.

I sip my Coors beer and look over at this self-confident delight of a man, contentedly puffing on a stub of a cigar as he stares up into the night sky trying to locate Ursa Major. I have no qualms about the adventure on which we are about to embark. In my bones I am convinced that a star is about to be born.

CHAPTER TWO

I turn off Lankershim Boulevard onto the Universal lot at 8:13. It's been a while since I last roused myself from a warm bed for an early morning studio visit but for Peter Falk I have made the effort. If he is nervous, I saw no signs of it at dinner last evening and this may be a quick show-the-flag visit and then back home to my typewriter to rescue Sam August from the viper pit hidden in the basement of power hungry industrialist Sven Norquist's Rocky Mountain chalet. Scotty, the custodian of the main gate, gives me a cheery hello and slips my drive-on pass underneath my windshield wiper. He's a holdover from the pre-MCA days. He may even have been around handing out parking passes to Lon Chaney when movies, like little children, were seen but not heard.

I park close to Stage 12 and jog up the stairs to the entrance. Inside I find the elaborate set that passes for Dr. Raymond Flemming's townhouse which he shares with his wife Carol. Sometime today Flemming, played by Gene Barry, will strangle her to death. Nina Foch is the unfortunate spouse. She will spend a lot of time lying motionless on the bedroom floor.

I spot Barry off to the side reading this morning's *LA Times*. No sign of either Peter or Nina Foch. The producer-director, Dick Irving, is in the middle of the set jawing with the cinematographer Ray

Rennahan. I sidle over to say hello as Ray walks off. Dick looks at me and glares. The last thing a director wants to see on a shooting set is some actor's agent or manager. They are always bad news. In my case, however, he knows better and the scowl turns into a smile. Dick is one of those guys who feels obligated to play tough even when he doesn't mean it which is most of the time.

"Worried about your boy, Joe? We're taking good care of him," Dick says.

"So he tells me. Just a social call, Dick. Nothing more. How do like his wardrobe?"

Dick snorts. "Not what I would have chosen but I've figured out real quick that Peter has great instincts and if walking around like a homeless bum is going to help his performance, fine by me."

"By the way," I ask, "where is he?"

"In wardrobe. I'm told he doesn't like his tie. He's finding a new one."

"Of course he is," I grin. "I'll see you later."

"Don't hurry," Dick says.

I head for the door. Wardrobe's two building's away. I'll touch base, wish the guy luck and then head back home. As I open the door and step out into the fresh air, I find another of Bowles & Bernard's meal tickets walking toward me. Bill Windom has been a client ever since 'To Kill a Mockingbird'. He's happy and so are we. Bill's one of the good guys. On this picture he has a supporting role as a district attorney.

"Joe! Wait up!" Bill calls out.

"I didn't know you were on call today, Bill," I say.

"Wardrobe fitting. By the way, our star is over there picking out neckties."

"So I was told."

"At last count he had nine of them draped over his arm. Picking them out isn't his problem. It's decision making that seems to have him buffaloed."

"He's very fussy," I say.

"I noticed," Bill replies. "Listen, Joe, I hear by the jungle drums that Ironside may be adding a new regular, an assistant district attorney."

"First I've heard of it," I say.

"Need I remind you I do lawyers very well."

"Of course you do, Bill. I'll have Zack Thorne check it out."

"Great. Nothing like a steady paycheck to calm the nerves."

"Your nerves don't need any calming, Bill. You're never out of work."

"I'm an actor. Anxiety comes with the territory."

"You know, playing second banana is okay but not if you want a rock solid career. Maybe it's time you thought about holding out for a show of your own."

"Ha! Delusions of grandeur. I'll tell Barbara you said that. Expect a nasty phone call around supper time."

"Okay, okay. Forget I mentioned it. I'll check with Sid on the Ironside thing." I'm talking about Sid Sheinberg, the number one guy in television development.

"Call me," he says, walking off.

"Right," I say.

He ambles over to the stage while I continue on to the wardrobe building where I learn that Peter has left the premises carrying a half-dozen neckties, having been unable to decide which of the six is right for the Columbo look.

"The man's a walking, talking derelict," Burt Miller says. Burt is the unit's wardrobe guy, an old timer and one of the best. "Last week I show him this fabulous light blue suit. He tries it on. A perfect fit. He hands it back to me and asks if I could please dye it a dirty brown to go with his raincoat which, by the way, I do not care to discuss."

"Don't fret it, Burt. Things will get really interesting if he ever comes in to pick out an overcoat."

I get a puzzled look from Burt as I head for the door.

When I get back to stage 12 Gene Barry and Nina Foch are rehearsing Nina's murder under Dick Irving's watchful eye. I spot Peter over by the craft services table showing Duffy Brown, the dolly grip, his selection of ties. I have known Duffy for more than ten years and in all that time I have never seen him in a tie. Nonetheless he does not seem shy about giving Peter his opinion. I walk over to join the conversation. Peter smiles in greeting.

"Joe, whatdaya say?"

"I say good morning and I need coffee. Hiya, Duffy."

"Morning, Mr. Bernardi."

"How's your boy?"

"Just made the Dean's list," Duffy says.

"Tell him hi for me."

"Will do."

He walks off as Peter thrusts his tie-laden arm in front of my face.

"Do me a favor, Joe. Take a look at these ties. Which one do you like?"

"They all look great to me."

"Yeah, but if you had to pick just one."

"I don't know. The blue stripe I guess."

"Nah, I don't think so," Peter says dismissively. "Duffy likes the orange one."

"Okay."

"Okay,what?"

"Okay, wear the orange one."

"I like the green one better."

"Then wear the green one."

Peter nods, holding it up to the light.

"I could do that," he says but I can tell he's agonizing "What about the blue polka dot?"

I can only shake my head.

"Peter, I love you dearly but I've got to be home for supper by six o'clock. Wear whatever makes you happy. Meantime, I am heading back to my typewriter which has been calling out my name ever since breakfast."

"Absolutely," Peter says. "I understand. Thanks for stopping by. I'm fine. Everything is terrific."

"Great," I say. "I'll call you later."

"That'll be good," Peter says.

I'm halfway to the stage door when I hear his voice calling after me.

"Joe, I hate to be a pest but one more thing. The red and black stripe. Whadaya think?"

I look back. He's holding it up hopefully.

"Go nuts," I say to him with a grin and then continue on my way.

As I step outside into the morning sun, I decide that Sam August, my dashing government agent hero, can wait for an hour or two. It's been at least two weeks since I've visited the guys on the 12th floor of the Tower and if Bill Windom is right and a recurring part is opening up on 'Ironside', I owe it to Bill to check it out. I hotfoot it over to the building, walk through the ground floor bank to the elevators and punch in 12. There is one other person on the elevator, a flamboyant writer-producer named Greg Lunsford, a hefty man in his late forties, invariably dressed in a three piece grey flannel suit with a Phi Beta Kappa key attached to a gold chain that hangs across his vest. His hair is sandy and worn long and his upper lip sports a bushy mustache that would make a British sergeant-major proud. Highly successful, Lunsford has three shows in the top 20 in the national ratings. All three are cookie-cutter procedurals each starring a has-been movie star teamed with a good looking young no-talent stud and made on the cheap. Quality is not a word that leaps to mind with a Lunsford series, still America loves them.

Lunsford and I are not close. No, that's not it. I hate the son of a bitch. He's got a reputation as a cocksman and he'll go after anything in a skirt just for the hell of it. Two years ago it was an assistant film editor named Jeannie. A great gal, fresh out of grad school, married to a paralegal named Toby. Long hours were tearing their marriage apart when Lunsford made a move on her. She never had a chance. She divorced Toby, giving up her year old daughter, and then Lunsford dumped her for some other chick. When she wouldn't let it go, Lunsford had her blackballed everywhere in town. Today she's back in Little Rock without her husband or daughter, living with her invalid mother.

"Joe," he says, throwing me his best insincere smile.

"Greg," I acknowledge, out of politeness.

"I've been meaning to call you," he says.

"Have you?"

The elevator cab starts to rise.

"David Janssen's been bugging me to make a deal for Sam August."

"I like David," I say, "but Sam's not yet ready for prime time television."

And I do like David a lot. He's a personable leading man who has just come off a long run in 'The Fugitive', a hugely popular series about an unjustly convicted man on the run from the police. But Walter Mirisch and I are still holding out for a motion picture vehicle for my brainchild. I have reservations about Janssen being able to carry a feature film though I could be wrong. However I am positive that Lunsford, a small screen mogul who squeezes nickels til the buffalos groan, doesn't have the chops for a major motion picture.

Lunsford regards me coldly.

"Big screen snobbery, Joe?"

"Not at all."

"I notice you didn't have any qualms about putting Peter Falk into that L.A. cop movie for NBC," he says.

"Different animal," I say. "Good script, good director, top notch production values, it has a chance to be something special."

"I could take offense at that," he says.

"Don't," I say. "It wasn't meant that way."

"Good to hear," he smiles. "Listen, if you're free Sunday why don't you join me on my yacht? I'll drag Janssen along and we can discuss the series idea. No obligation but it can't hurt to talk."

I smile inwardly. I am getting what's known about town as the Lunsford treatment. A day at sea on an eighty foot yacht, free flowing booze, cooperative female companionship and white powder for all in liberal quantities. More often than not network deals are made in such an atmosphere which explains Lunsford's success. If he could translate his sales technique into quality product he would be the most respected mogul in television history but unfortunately his relationship to top writers and directors comes nowhere near his kinship to Northern Lights, White Widow, Granddaddy Purple or other exotic strains of cannibis.

Just then the elevator stops and opens up onto the 12th floor, nerve center of Universal's television arm.

"After you," I say.

"I'm going up. Joe. A meeting with Wasserman. We're negotiating a film deal."

He smiles, having put me in my place. I step out of the elevator and the doors close. Greg Lunsford in the movie business. It boggles the mind. I start down the corridor toward Sid Sheinberg's office when Charlie Engel emerges from his office.

"Joe?"

"Good morning, Charlie."

Charlie is debonair with an ever-pleasant personality. He's one of several executives assigned to ride herd on Universal's television output.

"Here on business or just slumming?" he asks with a smile.

"I do all my slumming at Screen Gems. How've you been?"

"Great."

"I need a couple of minutes with Sid," I say.

"Not here," Charlie says. "He and Frank Price are on the back-lot trying to smooth troubled waters."

"The Virginian?"

"How'd you know?"

"Word gets around."

"Cobb could be a real pain in the ass but nothing like this. Dehner isn't cutting it and we've got insurrection on our hands. Anything I can help you with?"

"Maybe you can. I hear Ironside's thinking of adding an assistant D.A."

"It's being discussed."

"Something for Bill Windom?"

Charlie grins. "Doubtful. They're talking female."

"No good," I say. "Bill looks lousy in a dress."

"I imagine he does."

"Well, thanks anyway, Charlie. Good seeing you again."

I start off but Charlie stops me.

"Joe, tell Bill to sit tight. We're in talks with Sheldon Leonard about a half-hour project Bill would be perfect for."

"Tell me."

"Can't. Not yet but if and when we make the deal I think you and Bill should set up a meeting with Sheldon and his producer, Danny Arnold."

"Call me," I say.

"I'll put you at the top of the list."

I wink and toss him a little wave as I head back toward the

elevators. I've spent too much time away from Sam and his imaginary crises. If more schmoozing is needed, I'm going to leave it to Bertha. Soft soap is her specialty.

I'm home by eleven and find Bridget in the kitchen scrubbing pots. That's one thing about the Irish. They never met a pot that they didn't think needed just one more good scrubbing. Thoughtfully she's left the coffee in the percolator and I pour myself a mug before going upstairs. She also hands me a slip of paper on which there is a phone number and the name 'Haller'.

"He called three times, sir. A very anxious fellow. The third time he was less than polite so I hung up on him."

"As well you should have, Bridget," I say heading for the stairs with mug and message in hand.

When I'm settled at my desk I look at the note curiously. I know only three Hallers. One is Ernie, the cinematographer on 'Lilies of the Field' who retired two years ago after a stellar career that dated back to the silents. The second is his son Danny, also a cinematographer. I hardly know him and the thought crosses my mind that he may be calling with bad news regarding his Dad. This I dread. The third Haller is a man I have talked to only once in my life and have no desire to repeat the experience. Ever.

With trepidation I dial the number. Ernie is close to 70 years old, a lovely man, and I'm in no mood to hear bad news. After three rings, a woman answers.

"Hollywood Exposed," she says. "How may I direct your call?"

I hang up.

The third Haller is named Nate, a slimy excuse for a publisher, who digs up every imaginable kind of dirt for his monthly publication, widely read by equally slimy gossipmongers and voyeurs who cannot get enough bad news about the rich and famous of tinseltown. I have no idea why this man is calling me and I frankly don't want to know. Maybe he found out about that parking ticket

I picked up in Paso Robles thirteen years ago that I neglected to pay. Who knows? Who cares? I rip up the phone message and deposit the pieces in my waste basket.

CHAPTER THREE

It's half past twelve. I have been sitting at my typewriter for the past fifty minutes and in that time I have written exactly thirteen sentences, all of which I have crumpled up and tossed in the wastebasket. Sam is still hanging onto a heavy hemp rope as he dangles only a few feet above a swirling nest of poisonous snakes who are growing increasingly annoyed about missing their lunch hour. Matter of fact, so am I, but I am not going to let a little thing like writer's block keep me from finishing this scene. Sam has suffered a shoulder wound due to a lucky shot by Sven Norquist's Nepalese bodyguard, Guan Zook. Thanks to Sam's .44 Magnum, Zook is no longer among the living but this is small comfort to Sam who is suspended in midair, hanging on for dear life, his strength waning, unable to pull himself up to safety due to his shoulder wound. How long can he hold out? Better yet, how long can I hold out before I fix myself a ham and cheese sandwich?

My phone rings. Absentmindedly I pick up.

"Bernardi," I say.

"Don't you ever return calls?" comes a snarly voice with a noticeable Bronx accent.

"Who is this?"

"Nathan Haller and, pallie, I think you've got some kind of

death wish."

"I have nothing to say to you, Mr. Haller," I say, starting to hang up.

"Well, I have plenty to say to you, Bernardi, you and your pal, Falk. I suggest you listen."

I freeze when he mentions Peter's name. This can't be good.

"What about Falk?"

"Good. I've got your attention. Lunch at Musso's. One-fifteen. I'm buying. Don't be late."

"Not a prayer. I wouldn't be seen in public with you if I were on my deathbed."

"Then my office."

"Ditto."

"Too bad. Our next issue locks at six o'clock this evening and we hit the newsstands tomorrow morning at eight. I guarantee you won't be pleased. Good day, Mr. Bernardi."

"Wait!" I say, suddenly panicking. "The Malibu Pier."

"One fifteen?"

"Whatever jiggles your johnson."

"Come alone."

"You can be sure of that," I say, hanging up. I hesitate. Am I out of my mind? This guy is poison and yet the mention of Peter's name stopped me cold. Half the time Haller makes the stuff up, the other half consists of unsubstantiated rumors and backbiting by rivals, but true or false, the stink of a story in 'Hollywood Exposed' lingers for months. I owe it to Peter to find out what this slimy parasite is up to.

I hurry down the stairs and out to my car. If the traffic on Santa Monica Boulevard is light, I have plenty of time. Meanwhile, my stomach growls loudly as I keep thinking about that ham and cheese sandwich. I also keep thinking about Nate Haller and the little I really know about him except by reputation and the self-serving lies he puts out for public consumption.

According to his skimpy entry in 'Who's Who', Haller was born and raised in the Bronx where he worked briefly as a cub reporter for the *New York Post*, then joined the staff of Robert Harrison's 'Confidential' magazine, an East Coast based scandal magazine devoted to exposing the dark side of the rich and famous. Several years ago Haller quit and came west to start 'Hollywood Exposed', a monthly rag which was and continues to be a kissing cousin to his former employer. He has a battery of lawyers at his disposal and despite the renown and supposed power of some of his victims, no one has yet laid a glove on him. Now he has Peter Falk in his sights and I am nervous. Very nervous. I am not looking forward to this meeting. I turn off Santa Monica Boulevard onto the Pacific Coast Highway, heading north. Malibu is only a couple of minutes away.

The Malibu Pier is one of Southern California's most famous and most beloved landmarks. It's been around since the 1920's and through the years has been visited by tens of millions of tourists and locals alike. It boasts several decent restaurants and a dozen or more souvenir shops. Fishing is permitted off the end of the pier and immediately adjacent is Surfrider Beach, a favorite of surfers for generations. At one-fifteen the lunch crowd should be starting to disperse and I am not disappointed when I find a parking spot fairly close to the entrance. My hunger is becoming more pronounced but eating at a pier restaurant will entail eating across from Nathan Haller and this I will not do.

I find him sitting on a bench at the far end of the pier watching a couple of fishermen try their luck. He is a ferret of a man and even in slouched repose you can see there isn't much to him. Most likely in his fifties, he's balding and what's left of his hair has turned white. It could also use a good washing. He senses my approach and looks up. He screws his features into something that approximates a smile.

"Mr. Bernardi. Excellent. Come sit down," he says.

"No, thanks," I reply coldly. "I won't be here that long."

He shrugs. "I was hoping for a modicum of civility."

"Hope all you like. What's all this about Peter Falk?"

I remain standing and slowly edge around so that the afternoon sun is at my back and shining directly into Haller's eyes. Blinking uncomfortably he tries to shade them without success.

"You've discovered a major talent in Mr. Falk, Mr. Bernardi. I congratulate you. Barring any unforeseen circumstance you both should mutually prosper for many years to come."

"Get to the point, Haller. I don't have time to waste," I say.

Annoyed by the glare, he gets to his feet and walks over to the railing. A nearby fisherman is tossing chum on the water which suddenly starts whirling and churning. Unlike me, the flounder are having lunch.

"I'm doing you favor here, Bernardi, by getting your side of it. That rates me a measure of courtesy."

"Goodbye, Mr. Haller. Thanks for wasting my time," I say, turning on my heel and starting to walk away. He shouts after me.

"Your boy is a Communist," he says.

I stop and whirl back toward him.

"Bullshit," I say angrily.

"Maybe not now but he was and I can prove it."

"You mean that business years ago in Yugoslavia working on one of Marshal Tito's railroads?"

"You know about it," he says quietly, his bravado melting away.

"Of course I know about it. Peter and a babe named Sheila that he'd met in Paris went there looking for a little excitement. It was more Peace Corps than Afrika Corps—"

"I have proof. Papers signed by Tito himself—"

"You've got forgeries, pal, and you know it."

"I suppose you're going to tell me he was not a member of the

Marine Cooks and Stewards Union, a known Communist front."

"Of course he was. He had to be to get work just like every other seaman looking for a berth. Doesn't make him a Commie. Not even close."

Haller is starting to sweat now and he's stumbling over his words.

"Our material is very precise and well researched but we don't necessarily have to print it. At times we accept donations to our maintenance fund to save all parties involved a lot of aggravation—"

"Okay, now I get it. Journalism with a shovelful of blackmail thrown in, the better to keep your worthless rag financially afloat."

"You have it wrong, Bernardi—"

"No, I don't and to prove it, I'm going to let you talk to my lawyer. You tell him what you have and if he tells me to pay up, I'll pay."

"There's no need—"

"Sure there is. I know Ray would love to hear what you have. Ray. That's Ray Giordano, one of the top three lawyers in the L.A. area. I'm sure you've heard of him. Come on, Haller. There's a pay phone over there next to the bait shop. Let's hear what my buddy, Ray, has to say."

I'm getting ready to move but by now Haller has turned a half-dozen shades of white and grey.

"That won't be necessary," he says. "I need to confer with my editorial staff and reconfirm some of our data."

"You do that. And don't let the truth get in the way of your findings. That is not the way to run a putrid third rate scandal sheet."

He starts to walk away, visibly shaken, then turns back. His eyes bore into mine, spewing not fear but hatred.

"I'm not yet through with you, Bernardi. Believe me on that. Oh, yes, believe me very much."

With that he turns and walks away. I should be relieved. I'm not. I feel a chill. Something about that threat was very real and I'm pretty sure I don't want to find out what it is.

I wish I could remember why I was in such a hurry to get back to Sam August, the President's own special spymaster, who has thrice in three books saved the fifty states from total annihilation at the hands of some demented super villain. Sam is still hanging onto the rope mere inches above the poisonous nest of vipers, his energy waning, his hands chafed raw by the rope, and blood still seeping from his wounds. I stare at the half-typed sheet in the typewriter, then add a bit more color and tension to his predicament but who am I kidding? I am no closer to saving Sam's ass from the asps then I was at eight o'clock this morning. I am tempted to employ an ERB but I fight the impulse. I swore that I would never stoop that low and I am determined to honor that oath.

What, you may ask, is an ERB? It stands for Edgar Rice Burroughs, creator of Tarzan, and goes back decades to a period when the Tarzan books were serialized in a weekly magazine, a chapter a week, which were dutifully delivered by Burroughs in time for each week's deadline. This particular week had Jane being kidnapped by white slavers while Tarzan had accidentally fallen into a 12 foot deep elephant pit. Because of recent rain the walls of the pit were slippery mud and there were no protruding roots or any other sort of handholds. High above hungry predators were circling the mouth of the pit, anticipating dinner. The editors were agog. How in God's name would Tarzan escape to save Jane from the evil white slavers? Tarzan seemed doomed and so did Jane. The editors waited anxiously for the next chapter and when it arrived on print day, they tore the envelope open excitedly to learn what had happened. "Chapter Nine", they read and then: "Tarzan, safely out of the elephant pit, raced through the jungle to head off the white slavers who had taken his beloved Jane." So much for inventive problem solving.

The phone rings. I pick up.

"This is Joe," I say.

"I just want you to know, we had a terrific day, really terrific."
It's Peter Falk. "This guy Barry is a real oily bastard. I mean, not
Gene but his character. He's terrific. It's going great, Joe."

"I knew it would."

"I went with the green."

"What?"

"The tie. I went with the green."

"Good choice," I say.

"Yeah, I suppose but I really like that red and black stripe."

"Peter, forget the tie. Have you been talking to a guy named
Nathan Haller?"

"The magazine guy?"

"That's right."

"Why would I talk to him?"

"Well, don't and if he tries to contact you, refer him to me."

"What's going on, Joe?"

"Nothing I can't handle. Remember, no conversation with this
guy. Hang up and call me."

"I can do that but—"

"No buts, Peter. I used to do this for a living. Leave Nathan
Haller to me."

"You're the boss," he says.

"Right. When it comes to Haller, I am the boss."

We chat for another minute or two and then he gets called away
for rehearsal. Peter Falk a Communist. Yeah. And Santa Claus is
a Hari Krishna.

I turn my attention back to my typewriter and I am starting to
get really annoyed with Sam. Why is he always getting himself into
hot water and then expecting me to save his hide so he can save the
world? Several times in a fit of frustration I have considered dump-
ing Sam in favor of a super-intelligent spy trapped in an iron lung
who saves the world using brain power alone. I mentioned the idea

to my agent, Barry Loeb, who passed it on to my publisher who suggested that I immediately take the idea to Doubleday. So much for a not-so-dashing egghead hero.

I again stare at the page which stares back at me. Click. A notion flits across my brain. Hot water. Sure. Why not? The huge water heater suddenly malfunctions and scalding water spreads across the basement floor, into the viper pit boiling the little nasties where they squirmed. Wait. I need a trigger. Sure. Got it. It's no longer a nice day, it's pouring rain. A thunderstorm. Sheet lightning everywhere. The chalet is hit, a power surge disables the water heater, a pipe bursts, scalding water everywhere and boiled serpents litter the landscape. I nod in self-satisfaction. It isn't great but it beats the hell out of an ERB. In fact I'm kind of proud of myself.

I say as much to Bunny as we sit down to supper, not at home, but at Solley's Restaurant and Deli on Ventura Boulevard in Sherman Oaks. Tuesday is family night out and has been for years. At first it was Biff's All American Diner for spaghetti and hamburgers. Then Yvette, all of twelve years old, discovered Bella's Ristorante or, to be more accurate, she discovered Pietro, Bella's 17 year old son. Pietro lasted less than a year when Yvette got tired of flirting fruitlessly with this older man of her dreams and discovered a nice Jewish boy in the neighborhood. Half Jewish herself, she knew little of her heritage which is why Solley's has been our rendezvous for dinner for the past five months. Our housekeeper Bridget O'Shaugnessy is a marvelous cook but when it comes to gefilte fish and kreplach soup she is totally lost.

"I am so relieved you saved Sam's ass," Bunny says. "Whenever you run into a writers block you become impossible to live with."

"Nonsense," I say, "and for the record I never suffer from writer's block, only an occasional moment in plotting where I have to select from several options."

Bunny laughs.

"I'll put it on your tombstone," she says.

"What's beef tongue polonaise?" Yvette asks staring intently at the menu.

"No idea," I say.

"Me, either," Bunny chimes in. "Doesn't sound all that appetizing to me."

"That's because you're not Jewish," Yvette says. "I think I'll try it."

I love this phase Yvette is going through. Any day now I expect to find a picture of Moishe Dayan tacked to her bedroom wall.

We chat amiably about our respective days but when I mention Nate Haller, Bunny's face darkens.

"Disgusting little man," she mutters, taking a bite of her sauerkraut.

"You know him?" I ask.

"He stopped by the newspaper a few months ago wondering if we had anything in our files on Robert Mitchum. Mitchum used to live in the Valley when he was doing all those quickie Westerns before he hit the big time and got arrested on that marijuana charge."

"What did you tell him?"

"I told him to get lost. Our files are not open to the public and especially not open to muckrakers like him."

"He must have loved that."

"He stormed out of the office making threats at everyone including Benny Baxter's pet parrot which he keeps in a cage next to his desk."

"Like you said, gorgeous. A gem of a human being."

We arrived back home at eight-thirty. The tongue had turned out to be a little too Jewish for Yvette so after two bites she traded it in for roast chicken. Bunny opted for knockwurst and I settled for the brisket, a Solley's specialty. As soon as we walk through the door, Yvette makes a beeline for the phone in her bedroom to share the news of the day or at least the past two hours. Bunny heads for the kitchen to sort through the ice cream selection in the freezer and as for me, I spot a manila envelope on the table in the foyer. It is addressed to me and marked "Personal and Confidential." I open it.

The contents are several sheets of paper and a cover note which reads, tersely: "These are copies. I have the originals. Call me."

I flip the cover page and find Bunny staring up at me. Her eyes are hooded and bleary, her hair is a tangled mess, and she is holding a placard which identifies her as *Barbara Lesher, age 31, nka* (no known address). The bottom of the placard reads City of Moline, Illinois, Police Department. The date reads July 24, 1953. I flip to the next page. It is a xerox copy of a police report. The charges are vandalism, public drunkenness and lewd behavior.

I don't bother to look for some sign as to who sent this. I don't need to. And yes, I will call him, the first thing tomorrow morning. War has broken out. I didn't start it but by God, I will finish it.

CHAPTER FOUR

Eight o'clock Wednesday morning. I slept poorly last night. In fact I'm not sure I slept at all. Bunny is beside me, sound asleep, making those funny little purring noises I love so well. Gently I slip out from beneath the covers, grab my bathrobe from the back of the bathroom door, step into my slippers and head across the hall into the remodeled fourth bedroom that serves as my office. I sit down at my desk and open the bottom drawer, retrieving the envelope sent over last night by Nate Haller. Bunny doesn't know about it. There is no reason she has to. Whatever needs to be done to resolve this matter, I will do it.

I know all about Moline, Illinois. Also Elkhart, Indiana and Waterloo, Iowa. It was a dark time in Bunny's life as she fled across the country, emotionally crippled in the grip of alcohol, and in the company of a drugged out loser named Jake Fryman. Fryman had been a co-worker at *Collier's Magazine* in New York City. Divorced and dependent on heroin, Fryman used Bunny in every way possible from sex to sucking money out of her every chance he got. When management finally got fed up and fired her, Fryman quit his meaningless position and together they embarked on a month long odyssey throughout the Midwest. When he finally walked out on her in Ottumwa, Iowa, she was stranded without money or transportation. Desperate, she combed the truck stops for a guy who would listen to her sob story. It didn't take her long to find somebody. He lasted three days before he, too, had had enough and drove away alone from Independence, Missouri, while she was sitting in a jail cell awaiting arraignment on a charge of petty theft. Some time in the succeeding months, she discovered a Higher Power, surrendered herself to Alcoholics Anonymous and began to rebuild her life. Nine years ago she returned to me and we were married. Since then she has remained sober, a devoted and loving wife and equally important, a caring stepmother for Yvette. I love Bunny with more passion than ever before but I never want to relive those dark days when she was lost and I was helpless to save her. To dredge them up would be cruel and inhuman and whatever it takes, I will make sure that it doesn't happen. The past is dead and buried. Let it stay that way.

I slip the envelope back into the desk drawer, return to the bedroom and dress quietly so as not to wake Bunny. A few minutes later I am driving across town to the offices of 'Hollywood Exposed' on Vermont Avenue. I'm not sure what I am going to say or do but of one thing I am convinced: Nate Haller has to be dealt with. Whatever it takes, I think to myself. Whatever it takes.

The magazine occupies a suite on the third floor of an office building two blocks down from Hollywood Presbyterian Hospital. The building is ragtag and the name 'suite' is a misnomer. Haller and his crew occupy two adjoining offices connected by a door that leads from one to the other. I walk through the first door into a cramped anteroom that fronts two offices situated directly behind the reception desk. The woman at the desk is frumpy and her facial features approximate the sharp edges of a Bowie knife. She manufactures a smile as I walk up to her.

"Joseph Bernardi to see Mr. Haller," I say.

"Do you have an appointment?"

The name on her desk plaque reads Gladys Primm. I summon up my sincerest smile.

"No, Gladys," I say, "but trust me, I'm expected."

She frowns, trying to process what I've said. She can't.

"Mr. Haller's in a meeting," she says, "but I'll tell him you're here. Please take a seat."

I look around. There are three cushioned straight back chairs and a coffee table on which I spy a copy of this morning's Daily Variety. I sit and start to leaf through it as the receptionist picks up the phone and speaks quietly. When she hangs up she tells me that Mr. Haller is in an important meeting but will see me shortly. I nod my thanks and turn the page, suddenly surprised and saddened to see that Edna Ferber has died. One of the best known and most successful authors of the past five decades, she was 82 years old, and if she is remembered only for 'Showboat', her legacy will be secure for years to come. I skim the obituary. Her novels are legend. 'Cimarron', 'So Big', 'Giant'. Also 'Stage Door' and 'Dinner at Eight' on Broadway. Indeed she was a towering talent.

I glance at my watch. Sixteen minutes have passed. Haller's definition of 'shortly' differs considerably from mine. I toss aside the Variety and make a beeline for Haller's office. Gladys Primm says something which I ignore, turn the handle and step into the room.

The important meeting is in full swing. Haller is seated at his desk, a champagne glass in his hand. A statuesque blonde is sitting on the edge of the desk. She, too, is imbibing bubbly. Across the room a man is standing at a portable bar fixing himself what appears to be a bloody mary. When he turns at my intrusion, I recognize him right away. Six feet tall, barrel-chested with greying hair, Bart Kane is a detective working out of the Pacific Division of the LAPD centered in Venice. What's he doing here with this jackal? Something undercover? I stifle an impulse to acknowledge him and turn my attention to Haller.

"I got your message," I say to him.

"Yes, I wanted to clue you in as soon as possible. Your wife's story is too late for this week's edition. I have it scheduled for next week."

"Rethink that, Haller," I say.

"You may have bullied me on Falk, Bernardi. With your wife I have the goods."

"Don't count on it," I say giving the blonde a second look. Haller notes my interest.

"Claudia Hicks, my head of research. Claudia, Joseph Bernardi."

"I know who he is," she says dismissively.

"So you're the one who went diving into all those garbage pails," I say. "You clean up nicely, Miss Hicks. Too bad you can't keep yourself that way."

"Serving the public's right to know, Mr. Bernardi. Nothing more."

"How noble. With an altruistic attitude like that, you ought to run for Congress. Either that or swim a few laps in a shark tank. Either way you'll be right at home with your peers."

"You seem a little short on manners, Mr. Bernardi."

"I dispense them as merited, Miss Hicks."

"Now, now, children, let's not squabble," Haller cackles. "How may I help you, Joe? Shall we discuss the publication of your wife's sordid misadventures or perhaps you'd prefer to make a donation to our maintenance fund."

"Neither, Haller. I came to warn you. If one word of my wife's past appears in your publication, you will have bought more trouble than you can possibly deal with."

"I've heard idle threats before," Haller says.

"Not from me and I can assure you they are not idle. I know a little about the libel laws in this country and freedom of the press is not carte blanche to destroy lives just because you buy ink by the barrel. Since my wife is not a celebrity nor does she seek the public spotlight, there is such a thing as the public's compelling need to know. Also there is the matter of malicious intent which, considering our confrontation over Peter Falk, wouldn't be hard to prove. A good lawyer could force you into bankruptcy in a matter of months and I have a good lawyer. A very good lawyer. The best in the city, in fact. You've been warned, Haller. Proceed at your own risk."

I give him a withering look, feeling very much like Perry Mason on a good day, then turn and stride purposefully toward the corridor door, head held high. If they gave awards for sheer balls, I'd win hands down.

"Bernardi!"

I look back. He's framed in the doorway, eyes ablaze.

"Nobody walks away from me!" he screams.

"Guess again," I say. Out of the corner of my eye I can see Gladys, she of the tomahawk-like features, staring in disbelief.

"I'll ruin you and that bitch you married, see if I don't!"

I take a step toward him.

"You try and it'll be the last thing you ever do."

"You haven't got the guts," he sneers.

"Just keep telling yourself that, Haller," I say and then I'm out into the corridor and down the stairs, looking for much needed fresh air after that ludicrous and melodramatic exchange. I feel like a character in a bad B-movie. I've exited the front entrance and am halfway to my car when I hear a voice hailing me. I turn and Bart Kane is jogging to catch up with me.

"Well, Joe, if you had intended to piss him off, you succeeded admirably," Kane says, catching his breath.

"Glad to hear it," I reply.

He puts out his hand.

"Nice seeing you again," he says with a smile

We shake.

"Same here, Bart. So what's the play? You working undercover?"

He shakes his head. The smile has disappeared.

"No, just working. Chauffeur, bodyguard, that kind of thing."

"You're kidding."

"Wish I was. It's a job, Joe. I got a kid starting at UCLA in September."

"What happened to the cops?"

"Disability. Some kind of heart murmur. They forced me into early retirement which pays shit."

"You can do better than this guy," I say.

"I'm 47 with ulcers and migraines and I don't know how to do much outside of perp-walking guys into a station house. At least I can play the bills."

I shake my head in disgust, feeling sorry for the guy. Bad cops retire with beach houses a few miles south of L.A. Honest cops like Bart Kane grovel for part-time work to keep home and family together.

"What's with the woman?" I ask.

"Claudia? She's okay. Failed reporter, failed screen writer, failed divorcee. Acts tough to impress Haller but she isn't. Like me, it's a job."

I shake my head again.

"He must be paying you guys a helluva lot of money."

"We can only wish," Kane says ruefully. "Look, Joe, a word of warning. Heed it or not, up to you, but Haller is one vicious son of a bitch."

"I've heard."

"But you haven't seen," Kane says. "He's in it for the power and for the money, but more than that, he enjoys destroying people. If he's got something on your wife, he won't let up. It's what gets him out of bed in the morning."

"I've got a few weapons of my own," I say.

"Ray Giordano? I remember you two guys are close."

"You remember right, Bart."

Kane shakes his head.

"Ray might not be enough, Joe. You're not going to beat Haller with a rule book in your hand."

"Then I guess I'll have to try something else," I say.

"Yeah," Kane says. "Just don't get caught at it. Look, I gotta get back. Nice seeing you again, Joe, and uh, good luck." He turns and hurries back toward the building. I watch him go and then walk slowly to my car, wondering what that 'something else' might be.

It's early yet. Not even ten o'clock. I decide to drop by the office and pay the gang a visit. It's been a while since I've showed my face and I hear from Glenda Mae, once my good right arm, that my partner, Bertha, is morphing into a Brothers Grimm ogre. Since Glenda Mae always sees the best in her fellow man, this is troubling news and needs looking into.

I find Bert in Mallory Evans office griping about some insignificant glitch in the office paperwork. Mallory is our office manager charged with helming a smooth operation and she does a terrific job but right now she's sitting stoically at her desk, tears welling up, as Bertha administers an undeserved ass kicking. I grab Bert by the arm and drag her, protesting, to her private office.

"What the hell do you think you're doing?" she snarls at me as I plop her down on her office sofa.

"Trying to find out what's going on with you. You're too old for menopause so what the hell is it that's turned you into the Medusa."

"Who's been whining to you, Joe?"

"You want the whole list or just the ringleaders?"

She glares at me. I stare her down. Finally she averts her eyes.

"We have a great operation here, Bert, because we hire the best people but we can't keep them if you're going to keep acting like a psycho drill sergeant on mescal."

She nods but she won't look at me.

"What is it, Bert? What's going on?" I ask.

"Nothing."

I repeat myself more forcefully.

"What is it, Bert? And don't tell me nothing."

For a long time she remains silent and then she looks up at me.

"I'm losing my eyes," she says quietly.

"What? How?"

"Glaucoma."

"They can fix that."

"Sometimes. They should have caught it months ago."

"And they didn't because?"

"Because I've been buying dime store glasses because I haven't had the time or the guts to see my eye doctor."

"Damn," I say, partly out of anger for her stupidity but mostly because my heart is breaking for her. A fiercely independent woman, this is the last thing Bertha Bowles needs in her life.

"They're talking an operation," she says.

"Okay," I say.

"My condition is advanced and at my age there's a risk."

"You've never been afraid of risks."

She looks up at me, eyes blazing.

"I've never been 61 before. I've never had mild diabetes before. I've never had high blood pressure before."

And then she does something I've never seen her do. She starts to cry. I sit down beside her and take her in my arms and hold her close. She lets it go, all of it, and she is unable to stifle her sobs. We sit like that for the longest time and then she stops crying and gets up to pop a Kleenex from the box on her desk.

"Call your doctor, Bert. Schedule the surgery. Not next week. Now. I'll handle the office until you get back."

"No, Joe," she says, "your book—"

"My book will keep. You won't."

I get up and go to her and take her in my arms, holding her close, and I can feel her shaking uncontrollably.

"I'm scared, Joe. So scared."

"I know, Bert. I know."

CHAPTER FIVE

Bert finally composes herself and as I leave her office, she is on the phone with her eye doctor. We've agreed, the staff doesn't need to know a thing about this until the procedure is over. I have told her that I am ready to pitch in as early as tomorrow if necessary and as for Sam August he can jolly well wait until I am ready to once again deal with him. To tell you the truth I am getting a little tired of the guy always getting himself into impossible jams from which there is no escape and leaving it to me to clean up his messes. Maybe I should switch to children's books. Jill Marx, my daughter's mother, had the right idea. Whoever heard of a koala being mugged in a dark alley by a Soviet agent?

I'm at the elevators waiting for the next cab when Glenda Mae emerges from the office holding a pink phone slip. She hurries toward me.

"Whoever this is, she says it's important. She called here because she didn't know any other way to get in touch with you."

I take the phone slip from her and scan it: Claudia Hicks' home number. Call between noon and one.

"What's with Bertha?" Glenda Mae asks.

"Personal problems. I'll fill you in later. Meanwhile, Mallory's in charge and pass the word to show a little patience with Bertha."

"Whatever you say, boss."

The elevator arrives. I step inside.

"I'll call you later," I say. Usually this is accompanied by a smile and a wink but today the Bernardi charm is in short supply. Between Nate Haller and Bert's glaucoma I don't have much to be cheerful about. The doors close and the elevator starts down.

I'm home at eleven, grab some coffee and trudge up the stairs to my office. I have an hour to kill before I can call Claudia Hicks but I'll be damned if I am going to spend it with Sam August. I pick up my pages to date and stuff them into a desk drawer. Sorry, Sam, but right now you are one misery too many.

I pick up the phone and dial the Writer's Guild. I ask to be connected to Pauline and a moment later she comes on the line. Pauline Prosky is one of thousands of hopefuls who descend on Hollywood each year with dreams of stardom bubbling in their brains. Almost all will fail. Not talented enough. Not pretty enough, not connected enough, and in many cases not willing to do what has to be done to get noticed. To most people in the business, the idea of the casting couch is a joke. To many newcomers straight out of an Iowa high school, it's a nightmare. Pauline's one of the lucky ones. She had learned to type and take shorthand And she hasn't had sell her dignity to survive.

"Morning, Joe," she says. "Been a while."

"Too long," I agree.

"What can I do for you?"

"Claudia Hicks. Maybe television, maybe features. You probably don't have much."

"I'll check our files and get back to you."

"You're a princess."

"Of course I am. Remember what I said, Whenever you decide to dump the wife, I'm available."

"You're at the top my list."

"I'd better be," she says and hangs up.

I have to chuckle. She's a terrific gal but ill suited to the hurly burly of the Hollywood scene. She hangs on, taking lessons, auditioning for threadbare little theater productions, hoping for that one lucky break which will probably never come. Two years ago I offered her a job with the agency and she turned me down. She couldn't bear the thought of finding work for others when she couldn't find work for herself.

At ten minutes to twelve, Pauline calls back. Claudia Hicks has four Guild credits: two story credits that never went to script, an unsold 30-minute pilot about a wheelchair-bound psychiatrist and a 1964 episode of 'Mr. Novak', an hour series about a high school teacher. Since then, nothing. I thank Pauline for her help and make a mental note to have the office send over a dozen roses.

I wait until five past noon and then dial the number on the phone slip. She picks up almost immediately.

"Yes?"

"Joe Bernardi."

"I was hoping you'd get my message. I've been chatting with Bart. He says you're one of the good guys."

"I try."

"I called first of all to apologize—"

"Not necessary,"

"—and then to tell you you've blown it with Haller. I doubt he'd take your money now if you offered it. It's become very personal with him."

"If he prints anything, I'll destroy him and his magazine, Miss Hicks."

"Maybe yes, maybe no, but it'll be too late. You may have no idea what he's been able to dig up."

"You mean what YOU were able to dig up."

"Yes, that's right," she replies quietly.

"My wife and I have talked openly. I know everything."

"Everything? I seriously doubt it. It's dirty and demeaning and scurrilous and one of our staffers is already writing it up. At the very least this will cost her her job at the newspaper. Long term it's the kind of stink that never goes away."

She could be right. I think I know everything but maybe I don't. Maybe in an effort to spare me Bunny omitted some of the seamier details. Me, I don't care. What's over is over and the present is plenty good enough for me. But having her dark years exposed in a filthy rag like Haller's, that's something else.

"We should get together and talk," I say.

"Can't. I'm due back at the office by one-fifteen."

"I'll buy you dinner."

"What for?"

"I told you, conversation."

"And?"

"And what?"

"What else?" she asks.

"Nothing else," I reply.

"There's always something else, Mr. Bernardi," she says.

"Would you feel better if I asked my wife to join us?"

Silence from her end, then:

"There's a chink place in West Hollywood on La Cienega. The Yellow Dragon."

"I'll find it. What time?"

"Seven."

"And should I bring my wife?"

"Up to you but I wouldn't."

"Then I won't. See you at seven."

I hang up. It's going to be a long afternoon.

I last until two o'clock and then I can't take it any more. I go downstairs and notify Bridget that I have an important evening meeting and will not be home for dinner. I need to get out of here before Bunny comes home lest I somehow slip and give myself away. Tonight in particular Bunny doesn't need to know who I'm having dinner with and why.

I drive to the office and get hit with good news the minute I walk in the door. Bert has been making the rounds, apologizing to everyone for her boorish behavior and the atmosphere is practically festive. I make my way to her office and shut the door behind me. She tosses me a huge smile.

"The day after tomorrow. Eight in the morning. Dr. Crimmens is delighted."

"Good for him and good for you," I say.

"The procedure is pain-free and not quite as dangerous as I first thought. He's going to do it in his office and then send me home to recuperate. I've already arranged for a registered nurse around the clock. The doctor says I won't need her but I'll feel better if someone is close by."

"Then by all means."

"For about a week, no driving, no reading, bending or heavy lifting. I forgot to ask him about television. For six weeks my vision will be a little blurred but then it should return to normal."

"And that's when you'll come back to work," I say.

"Oh, no, I'll be back long before that."

"No, you won't, even if we have to change the locks. Now don't you feel a little silly, getting yourself all worked up for no good reason?"

"I'm taking the fifth," she says.

"Of course you are," I say." Why spoil a perfect record of never being wrong about anything, no time, no place and no how."

She starts to say something, then breaks out laughing. I do, too.

So, today is Wednesday. Friday morning she undergoes the surgery and I babysit the office in her stead, Two days of weekend and then it's Monday. Despite my protests she'll be back here at her desk, shouting orders and cracking the whip. Just like old times.

I find the Yellow Dragon without difficulty, park in the street and walk in at two minutes to seven.Claudia is sitting at a booth in the rear nursing a pot of hot tea. I slide in across from her. She smiles.

"No trouble finding the place?"

"None."

"Shall we order?"

"Let's see the material, If it's bogus, I may not be staying long."

She hesitates, then picks up a manila envelope on the seat beside her and slides it across the table. I open it and start to scan the material. She won't meet my eyes but stares into her tea cup, taking an occasional sip. Finally I slip the papers back into the envelope and slide it back to her.

"No surprises here," I say.

She puts the envelope back on the seat and then stares at me quizzically.

"You're a most unusual man," she says.

"Am I?"

"Most men couldn't deal wth something like this."

"I love my wife," I say.

"Obviously."

"What are we doing here?" I ask.

"Most donations to the maintenance fund run five to ten thousand. From you he'll want more. A matter of pride. You're looking at twenty-five thousand minimum.'

"I thought you said he wouldn't take my money."

"I said I doubted it. I assume you can pay."

"I can but I won't."

"Once he publishes it'll be too late."

"Then I'll find a way to stop him from publishing."

"How are you going to do that?"

"I'm not sure. I know people who could threaten him in such a way that he'd be in fear for his life."

"And if that didn't work?"

"Make no mistake, Miss Hicks. I will stop at nothing to protect my wife."

"That's what Greg Lunsford said."

"What's Greg Lunsford got to do with this?"

She blanches, wishing she could take it back.

"I'm sorry. I shouldn't have mentioned his name." She looks at me nervously, "I spoke out of turn. I shouldn't even be here talking to you. Please."

"I don't remember reading any dirt on Lunsford."

"No, you didn't. Leave it at that."

She stares at me without looking away. I get it. Lunsford paid.

"Stop at nothing," she says. "A remark like that could be misconstrued."

"Really?" I say. "I thought I was quite clear. Did he send you here?"

"No."

"To feel me out? Find out where I was headed?"

"I said no!" she says angrily.

"Okay," I say.

The waiter comes and we order won ton soup, one beef dish, one chicken and some fried rice. I help myself to hot tea and we chat waiting for our food. She's from a small town in Nebraska and valedictorian of an equally small high school. She also edited the school paper and starred in the school play, The competition wasn't tough. The graduating class numbered 56. After graduation she married the town barber's son for a quick cup of coffee and then lammed it out of there when she caught the guy in the sack with the town manicurist. She landed in L.A. and hooked up with a has-been TV writer who showed her a few screenwriting tricks.

When he died of an overdose she bounced around for a couple of years, picking up an assignment here and there before answering a want ad for "˜Hollywood Exposed'.

"Tell me about the script you wrote for Mr. Novak." I say. She cocks her head curiously. I've caught her by surprise. "You're not the only one who can do research, Miss Hicks."

"It was a pretty good episode. By that time I knew what I was doing."

"Yet you quit."

"Had to. This guy, a second assistant director, he got me in the door. After I handed in the final script he was telling everyone that it wasn't my work, that he'd written most of it. I called him on it but most people believed him. After all, who was I? The Writers Guild arbitrators weren't fooled. They assigned me full credit but the damage was done. The twerp had me blackballed all over town. That's when I answered Haller's ad."

I nod.

"You know I never really read 'Hollywood Exposed.'"

"It's all right," she says with a smile. "Everybody says that."

"But I mean it," I protest. "Doesn't mean I haven't picked up a copy now and then. Seems to me the really juicy stories were written by a guy named Faraday."

"Bill Faraday. He and Nathan had a falling out a few months ago. I replaced him. I may not be around much longer myself."

"Oh?"

"Nate preferred the way Bill dug out the dirt."

"And how was that?"

"Bill had an arrangement with several big name biographers around the country, ghost writers and such, mostly in L.A. and New York. They'd write bios or puff pieces on assignment for a big name magazine like the *Post* or the *Atlantic Monthly* and when they dug up something ugly about their subject, they'd sell it to Bill for big bucks. They weren't violating their contracts because what they learned the publication wouldn't print. Family mags are like that. Nate always gave his targets a chance to contribute to the fund and mostly they paid."

"Including Lunsford," I say staring at her hard. I know she'd like to look away but she can't or won't.

"Yes, including Lunsford," she says finally.

"And what did Faraday have on him?"

"I don't know. Faraday was gone by the time I arrived and Nathan keeps all the fund material carefully hidden from the rest of us." She sips some tea, by now almost certainly cold. "He's especially secretive about Lunsford."

"And just what is it about the way you operate that Nate Haller doesn't like?"

"I'm a goody two shoes. I like to pepper my stories with the truth. Some philandering movie star humping some starlet newly arrived from Sheboygan, he's fair game. Ditto crooked lawyers, incompetent doctors and thieving politicians. But raw fiction about decent people, that's for the funny papers."

"You know, lady," I smile, "I like your style."

The food comes and we dig in, chatting about nothing of consequence. Claudia Hicks is a survivor in a sea of victims. She reminds me of Pauline Prosky. It's obvious she hates where she works and what she has to do to survive but she accepts it as less degrading than her other options.

We're finishing up when I spot a familiar face across the room. Jesse Simmons, a young writer-producer has just been seated by the hostess and is obviously waiting for a dinner companion. He's based at Paramount and has just sold a dramatic series to ABC for next season. I hear he's staffing up. I wave to him and after a moment he looks up and I catch his eye. He waves back. I beckon him too join us. He hesitates, then puts down his menu and walks toward us across the room.

We shake and exchange greetings.

"I'm waiting for a friend, Joe," he says and I can guess who it is. Jesse is reputedly in a new relationship with a casting director at Screen Gems.

"Not a problem," I say. "I just wanted you to meet Claudia Hicks, a terrific young writer you probably never heard of. Claudia, Jesse Simmons. Jesse, Claudia." They shake amiably. "Claudia was just getting started about four years ago. Wrote a brilliant Mr. Novak when suddenly her mother became gravely ill and she had to return to Nebraska to take care of her."

"Bad break," Jesse says.

"Thankfully," I say, "she passed on last week dying peacefully in her sleep, free of pain. A blessing."

"Yes, a blessing," Claudia says, playing along.

"Claudia's back to resume her career and we're here discussing a lot of options. Anyway, Jess, when I saw you, it just hit me that you might be looking for talent for your new show."

"I am."

"Correct me if I'm wrong but it's about an idealistic young lawyer?"

"Devlin for the Defense," Jesse says.

"Seems to me there's not a nickel's worth of difference between an idealistic lawyer and an idealistic high school teacher."

"Probably not." He looks over at Claudia. "Are you free tomorrow?"

"I could be," she says.

"Great." He hands her his card. "Call my girl early in the morning and we'll set up something for the afternoon. I want you to meet my story editor, Ben Fowler. Any problem?"

"None. And thanks."

"No. And thank YOU," Jesse says with a smile and then spots

his date, a good looking young man with blonde hair worn stylishly long, being seated at his table. His name eludes me but I recognize him. He plays a rookie cop on a second year series starring an old warhorse from the old days at MGM.

"Tomorrow, then, Claudia," Jesse says, getting up, "and Joe, nice seeing you." He hurries back to his table. Claudia watches him go and then looks at me.

"Thanks," she says.

"My pleasure."

"Why did you do it?"

"Because I could," I tell her with a smile, then reach over and take her hand in mine and give it a squeeze.

CHAPTER SIX

Thursday morning. I don't need tea leaves to tell me that today will be interminable, a 72-hour day at the very least. Sam August is on my manure-list and I refuse to write one more sentence until I have come to terms with his chutzpah. I am not sure how many more times I will be able to save his self-serving ass from impossible predicaments. My overworked brain is starting to suffer from delusions of inadequacy. I am also concerned about Bert's surgery tomorrow morning and feeling very helpless. And, too, I worry about what that shark Nate Haller is up to, not to mention that I am anxious to hear from Claudia Hicks about her meeting with Jesse Simmons and his story editor.

I check my watch. Ten to eight. Bunny's already up and out of the house. Staff meeting at the newspaper. It's not too early for my first call so I dial out.

"Clausen," he says.

Mick Clausen is invariably at his desk no later than seven thirty and often even earlier. L.A.'s most successful bail bondsman, he knows the underbelly of the city like a Hollywood Madam knows the men who run it. He is also married to my first wife, Lydia, and despite this (or maybe because of it), he is probably my best and most trusted friend.

"It's me," I say.

"Aha, Joe Bernardi calling before eight in the morning. What can this be? What does he want? Because he sure hasn't called to ask about the crabgrass that is strangling my front lawn."

"Nate Haller," I say.

"Oh, great," Mick responds, "it's bad enough you occasionally have me going after the mayor or some city councilman, now I am supposed to take on Lucifer."

"Information, Mick. That's all."

"And what are you up to now, my friend?"

I tell him.

"Jesus Christ," he sputters. "Nothing with you is ever easy, Joe. What do you need from me?"

"Anything and everything. If he was caught necking with his sister when he was ten years old, I want to know about it."

"By when?"

"Yesterday."

"Silly me," Mick laughs mirthlessly. "Why do I even bother to ask? And I'm doing this why?"

"Because the bastard's got something on me—correction, something on Bunny—and I want to return the favor."

"I see. You get something out of Haller's past that's ugly enough and he won't print what he has on Bunny."

"Something like that."

"And what if he doesn't care, Joe? A man like that has no reputation to protect. He might just laugh at you."

"Then I'll have to activate Plan B."

"Which is?"

"Better that you don't know, Mick. Accessory before the fact. That sort of thing. Can you help?" I ask.

"I can try but it's going to cost me lots of overtime."

"Thanks, Mick," I say. "Greater love hath no man than to lay down his P&L statement for a friend."

"Fuck off," Mick snarls as he hangs up.

A good sign. Now I know he'll go all out for me.

Next up. Greg Lunsford but for him it's much too early so I wander downstairs in search of breakfast. Bridget is puttering around the kitchen and when I appear she looks at me askance. Bathrobe and underwear, a day old stubble and ratty slippers on my feet. She suspects the worst, that I will stay home all day, ordering her about for beer and sandwiches and then more beer. When she hears I am setting up appointments all day long, she relaxes long enough to scramble me some eggs. Bridget is priceless. Apparently the less she sees of me, the more she seems to love me. I can hardly imagine the euphoria she'll feel when, at last, I cross my final t and dot my final i.

I'm back upstairs at ten and call Greg Lunsford at Universal. His girl doesn't recognize my name and doesn't want to put me me through so I tell her I'm calling from Jack Webb's office and it's most important I talk to Mr. Lunsford immediately.

"What have you got going with Webb?" he asks when he comes on the line?"

"Nothing," I say, "but your girl wasn't about to put me through if I were nothing more than an Oscar-nominated screenwriter."

Lunsford laughs.

"I'll have to talk to her about that. What can I do for you, Joe?"

"How about lunch? Are you free?"

"This is an unexpected invitation."

"We have things to discuss," I say.

"Like a television series based on Sam August?"

"Sure, that, too, but what we really need to talk about is Nate Haller."

There is a long silence on his end of the phone. Then he says, "I have nothing to do with Haller."

"Sure you do. You paid him off and I don't care why but now

he's after me and I think the two of us and maybe a couple of others who have been victimized might join forces and put this guy out of business."

"I'm sorry if you're on his radar screen, Joe, but as for the rest of it, I don't know what you're talking about."

"When's the second payment coming due, Greg? And the third? Now that you're on the hook, he's not going to stop."

"And I said, I don't know what you're talking about. If you want to discuss Sam August, fine. Otherwise, I pass."

"You're making a mistake," I say.

"Make 'em all the time, Joe, but I'm always able to slough them off onto the people who work for me. But, hey, maybe in a few months, you may change your mind about Sam. If you do, call me. My door's always open." He hangs up.

With a sigh I return the receiver to the cradle. Now I not only have no ally in my fight with Haller, I also have no lunch date. I suppose I could call Phineas but the moment it occurs to me, I discard it. Phineas writes the entertainment column for the *L.A. Times* and his oversized nose can smell out a story from a hundred paces. If I want to keep my troubles with Nate Haller secret, I need to keep a lot of distance between me and Phineas. Glenda Mae, however, is a different story. I dial the office and a few moments later, I've got her where I want her.

"What do you need?" she asks without wasting a breath on the niceties of phone etiquette. I'm as obvious as the wart on the end of the Wicked Witch's nose.

"Your unrivaled skills as a detective," I say smoothly.

"Oh, Christ, this is going to be a beaut," she mutters.

"Nothing you can't handle, sweet thing," I say. "Some time back there was this huge spread on Greg Lunsford. Don't remember the publication but I need to talk to the writer, whoever it was."

"No problem," Glenda Mae says.

"And I need this right away, gorgeous. Tomorrow or even 'later this evening' aren't going to cut it."

"Where are you?"

"Home."

"Okay, I'm on it or at least I will be as soon as you get off the damned phone."

"Love you, baby," I say.

"Of course you do," she says, hanging up.

I lean back in my chair and relax just a wee bit. Glenda Mae is a can-do girl and I know she'll come through. Meanwhile I have a host of other things to deal with, not the least of which is my bothersome hero who is injecting himself more and more into the plotting process. I wonder if Ray Chandler had to put up with this sort of crap from Philip Marlowe.

With increasing irritation, I open my desk drawer and remove the current adventure of my intrepid hero. I scan the pages, sometimes feeling euphoric, more often displeased. I grab a blank sheet of paper from the shelf behind me and slip it into my typewriter. I begin to write:

> Sam rummages in the bottom drawer of his desk and withdraws his prized pearl-handled.45 automatic. He pulls the slide, seating a round, and after a momentary pause places the barrel of the pistol in his mouth. Without hesitation, he pulls the trigger. His head snaps back, what's left of it, as blood and brains splatter onto the wall behind him. His body slumps in the chair. The weapon falls to the floor. At midnight, three hours from now, the island of Cyprus will explode and what remains will slip quietly into the Mediterranean. Rupert Montenegro, the evil munitions baron, will have succeeded and Sam August is no more.

I stare long and hard at the paragraph I have just written. I feel good all over as if I'm soaking in a hot tub with a beer buzz on and nothing bothers me and nothing can get to me. Then I take another long look at my pipe dream and toss it into the wastebasket.

"Not now, buddy," I mutter. "Not yet. But one of these days."

The phone rings. I pick up.

"Mr. Bernardi?" A pleasant woman's voice.

"Yes," I reply.

"Please hold for Mr. Sheinberg."

I have nothing better to do so I hold for Mr. Sheinberg. He comes on the line almost immediately."

"Joe!" Warm and jovial. He wants something.

"Hi, Sid."

"I'm not interrupting anything, am I?"

"No, I just finished killing off my hero and I'm going to leave him that way at least until tomorrow morning when I expect an apology for being such a jerk."

I hear him laugh. He may have gotten it, maybe not. With Sid you're never sure.

"I know this is late notice but how's your lunch look?" he asks.

"I can free myself up," I reply. For the number three man at MCA? You bet I can.

"Great. We'll be watching Peter Falk's dailies at 12:30. I think you'll be pleased. I know we are. After that, we can talk business over lunch in the private dining room."

"Looking forward to it," I say.

At twelve thirty I am sitting in one of Universal's many screening rooms, preparing to watch film of the scenes that were shot yesterday. Sid Sheinberg is at my side. Others in the darkened room include Frank Price and Charlie Engel, Ralph Winters, head of casting, and Monique James who runs the talent development department which has already spawned the likes of Clint Eastwood and Rock Hudson and Tony Curtis. Also on hand are Richard Levinson and William Link, *Columbo*'s creators, the two buddies from Philadelphia, who have been writing together since junior high school.

The lights dim, the film rolls. Gene Barry, playing a wealthy psychiatrist, enters his swanky condo, returning after a business trip. Ordinarily his wife would greet him but he knows she won't because shortly before flying away, he strangled her, leaving her dead on the bedroom floor. Peter Falk as Lt. Columbo emerges from the bedroom and introduces himself and then explains to a 'bewildered' Gene Barry that his wife is dead, apparently murdered by a burglar. Barry is 'shocked' and 'devastated'. Columbo, soft-spoken and unfailingly polite, asks Barry how he knew? Knew what, Barry asks. That she was dead, Columbo counters. You see, Columbo explains, when I walk in the house, I call out to the missus, "Hi, I'm home!" or words to that effect, I mean, it's just the natural thing to do, but the funny thing is, you walked in the door and you didn't say anything. You didn't call out, nothing like that and I find that strange, Columbo observes, and then he is off and running, scratching his head, looking for a pencil, trying to take notes, commenting on the decor, relating an incident that happened to his cousin Guido's son, Anthony. And all the while, Barry is obviously wondering how this dunce ever got to be a police detective. Barry is excellent as the suave and conniving killer but Falk steals every frame of film with his lovably disarming performance. I don't need a scorecard to know that something very special is happening.

My assessment is confirmed forty minutes later in the executive dining room just off the commissary. A soft-spoken slim six-footer with an easy smile but a somewhat absent-minded aura about him, Sid Sheinberg is slathering butter on a baked potato when he says, "NBC is ecstatic. They're ready to commit to 13 episodes for next fall's schedule."

"Wow," I say quietly. "Off of one day's set of dailies?"

"Doesn't happen often, Joe," Sheinberg says. "What do you think?"

"I think it's terrific, Sid, but I'm not so sure about Peter. He does not speak lovingly about his work experience with O'Brien." Two years ago Peter starred as lawyer Danny O'Brien in 'The Trials of O'Brien" which tanked after only 13 episodes despite excellent critical acclaim. I have a strong suspicion it is not an experience he is anxious to repeat.

"I can understand that," Sid says. "O'Brien was an excellent show. It should have succeeded and I have no idea why it didn't. But Columbo is something else again, Joe. He could easily become an iconic character like Hercule Poirot or Sherlock Holmes or Sam Spade. Talk to him, Joe."

"Of course I'll talk to him. I just wanted you to know where his head is if he says no."

We chat easily through the remainder of lunch, Sid subtly buttressing his arguments for Peter's participation and me, trying to talk about anything but. I have nothing concrete to say until Peter and I have a conversation and Sid knows it. Still he hangs in there, swinging hard, making sure I am aware of every inducement the network and the studio can offer to get him to sign up.

It's past two o'clock when Sid and I walk out of the commissary and shake hands. I promise to get with Peter right away and after I do, Sid will be my first call. Sid smiles. Can't ask for more, he says and heads off toward the Black Tower. I begin to walk back toward Stage 6 where I parked my car when I feel a tug on my arm. I turn and look into the furious visage of Nate Haller.

"Now what, Bernardi? You spying on me?" he hisses.

"I don't know what you're talking about."

"No? You're saying you don't have people poking around my building, asking questions about me to my neighbors?"

"If I do, Haller, you've got a hell of a nerve complaining. Digging for crap in a dung heap is the only reason you prosper."

"Stay out of my personal life, Bernardi."

"Sure, how about if you stay out of mine."

We're toe to toe, eyeball to eyeball, although I have to stoop a little as I have him by a good seven inches. Our voices are raised and we're starting to attract a crowd.

"The world needs to know about the lush you married, Bernardi, and they're going to. There's no deal, not for all the money in the world. You hear me?"

He grabs my arm and instinctively I shove him away. He loses his balance and falls to the asphalt. I hear a woman gasp. I look around. People are staring at us. One of them is Denny Crowe, a black actor who specializes in playing teen gang members even though he's 26. He's a nice enough guy but he doesn't work all that much. He stares at me with mouth agape.

"You son of a bitch!" Haller screams, struggling to get to his feet.

"You're through, Haller," I say. "Maybe not tomorrow or next week but I'm going to put an end to you whatever means it takes." I look around at my audience. I can imagine how it appears. Virile six footer versus a short balding old man but I don't give a damn about appearances. I point to Haller and pantomime downing a slug of whiskey. "Pathetic," I say, shaking my head sadly and then I continue on my way.

I'm angry, really angry, and I came close to punching Haller out. I guess common sense saved me from doing something really dumb and now as I sit behind the wheel of my car I can feel the rage melt away. I meant what I said. I am going to put a stop to this man but a punch in the nose won't do much and can only buy me more trouble. No, the more I think about it, the more I'm sure I will win by taking Haller down at his own game.

Now is not a good time to approach Peter with NBC's interest in a *Columbo* series. He's on location in Pasadena and besides I need time to think about the pros and cons of NBC's offer. Better that I drive downtown to the Civic Center and find out from Mick what progress is being made, if any, in exposing Nate Haller for the evil bastard that he is.

CHAPTER SEVEN

When I drive away from the Universal lot, I could easily head for home and a much needed nap in the chaise on the back patio. I choose not to because I am bedeviled by something called the 'Protestant work ethic' which is odd because I am Catholic (failed). Instead I head straight for the Civic Center and the nearby offices of Mick Clausen, Bail Bondsman. Haller's mention of his neighbors being queried tells me the snoop job is well under way and curiosity is getting the better of me. Not that I expect much, not after a few paltry hours, but you never know. Mick's people are the best.

When I walk through the door I see that Lydia, my ex now married to Mick, is working the counter while Mick is poring over some paperwork in his office. I peer into the back room where two of Mick's best operatives, Kim Overmeyer and Tony Romano, are on separate phones. talking and taking notes. Kim sees me and smiles, giving me the high sign. The counterattack is in progress.

Lydia is busy with a elderly woman seeking help for a rebellious grandson but catching my eye, nods in Mick's direction. I smile and head back to Mick's office. He sees me coming and waves me in.

"It's not much," he says, gesturing to a chair, "at least not yet, but it could be big."

"Tell me," I say, grabbing a bottled water from a cabinet and then sitting.

"Haller's not his real name," Mick says.

"That's big," I say.

"Sure is. According to the Social Security Administration he was born in the Bronx in 1918 under the name Nathan Halperin, lived there for sixteen years before he dropped out of high school and left the city in 1934 for parts unknown. The next sighting was in 1940, Mobile, Alabama, where he found work on a tramp steamer hitting the ports all around the Caribbean. He was a rowdy and a boozer and the cops were always picking him up for bar fights and disturbing the peace. He hung around with a kid named Irish so-called because he hailed from Dublin, Georgia, but no one knew his real name. He might have been eighteen or nineteen, just out of high school, not a big talker. And then one night there was a brawl at one of the waterfront bars and a man was killed, an out-of-town cop on vacation with his girlfriend. The next morning Haller and Irish dropped out of sight. That afternoon a woman came to the police station to report that her roomer had not only stiffed her for two weeks rent but he'd also stolen her car. His name, she said, was Garry Leden but his friends, the few he had, called him Irish."

"So Haller and the kid Leden killed this guy in a bar brawl and split," I say.

"Probably but nobody in the bar was talking. Seems the out-of-town cop was a loud mouth jerk who was asking for trouble."

"Got it."

"Anyway three days later the landlady's car winds up in Jackson, Mississippi, with no sign of Irish or his buddy Nathan Halperin. Five months go by. The bar brawl is forgotten, the out-of-town cop is forgotten and it's Brownsville, Texas, and Nathan Halperin, now known as Nathan Haller, is writing drivel for a weekly newspaper. At 33 with bad eyesight he is not draft bait. Not so 'Irish' Garry

Leden who feels the hot breath of the Dublin, Georgia, draft board on his neck and starts to go by the name of—" He hesitates, waiting for me to finish the sentence.

"Gregory Lunsford," I say in a moment of brilliance.

"The one and only. He is situated in Tulsa writing 30 minute radio dramas for a local Tulsa station and after that the trail on 'Irish' goes cold. As for Haller, he leaves Brownsville for a better job in Houston, an after-dark reporter for the metro section which includes a lot of murders, rapes and robberies. He must have felt right at home. When he learned that Confidential was paying good money for salacious stories about celebrities, he fired off a couple of first hand accounts from a buddy who was a steward on a Caribbean cruise line. One involved a well known actress in the middle of getting her fourth divorce. The other was about an elderly male author of children's books traveling with his 12 year old nephew except that the author didn't have a nephew. Within a month Haller was summoned to New York and hired as a Confidential staff writer. The rest you know. A few years in New York learning the game and then westward ho to start his own vile publication."

"Nice work, Mick. Thanks," I say.

"Don't thank me. Kim's a real birddog. Give him another day or two and he'll have Haller's history out there for all the world to see."

"Including a healthy handful of dirt," I say.

"One can only hope," Mick says.

"Haller goes to press Monday, Mick. I need something to threaten him with—anything—even if it's only half baked."

"I hear you, Joe. If it's there, Kim will find it in time. That's a promise."

My heart is not so heavy as it was as I head for home. It's a quarter past six and I left Kim still working diligently, checking merchant marine sources for the years 1934 through 1940. Mick is right. If there's something to be found, Kim will find it. I just hope he finds it in time. I'm intrigued by the idea that Haller and Lunsford might have known each other twenty five or thirty years ago. It might be hard to prove and even if true, what does it mean? I've also gotten good news from Glenda Mae. The article lauding Lunsford appeared a few weeks ago in a weekly edition of Variety which occasionally does personality profiles on mass media moguls. The piece was written by a guy named Brett Klinger whom I had actually met once when he was trying to find a home for a screenplay he had written with his gal pal at the time. Glenda Mae has supplied Klinger's phone number and warned me that he is out of town, expected back home this evening before midnight. I seem to remember that Klinger is quiet and polite, a man of words and not action.

Deep down I am not afraid of Nate Haller. I have done nothing in my life to be ashamed of and if the slime in his upcoming issue concerned only me, I wouldn't give him a dime. But this isn't about me and I am not going to let Bunny suffer public humiliation if I can do anything to prevent it. I have enough money to meet any demand Haller might make and as for his pompous pronouncement that in my case, he will not accept a donation to his so-called maintenance fund, I instinctively know that for Haller, money is not just paramount, it's the only thing that matters.

I am greeted at the door by Yvette who jumps into my arms and gives me a huge hug and a kiss. If I didn't know better I'd suspect that she wanted something. If so I'll deal with it later when my aching back has returned to normal. I hug Bunny, aiming a kiss at her lips but they miss the target when she averts her face. Uh-oh. What have I done now?

"There was a phone call for you about a half hour ago, Joe. Someone named Claudia. She sounded young, very young, a member of one of your high school fan clubs perhaps."

She's smiling but the words are frostbitten.

"Oh, sure. Claudia Hicks," I say as if she has been a close friend of the family for years. Bunny is not fooled.

"I have the number right here," she says holding up a phone slip, "on the unlikely chance you don't know it by heart."

"I don't," I say, snatching the slip away from her. "I'll take it in the library where I can speak to her without being overheard by jealous wives or other unworthy human beings."

Two can play at that game so I do but I know Bunny's real aim is to push my buttons until I squeal for mercy. It's her way of saying, this is my man so hands off unless you want a handful of fingernails in your eyes. I counter by trying to frustrate her prying ways and finally we both end up laughing. When Yvette is witness to one of these exchanges, she is totally bewildered but soon she'll be at an age when a little gamesmanship is part of the spice of life.

"I'll tell you all about her over dinner," I say.

"You'd better, chicky baby," she replies, another of her terms of endearment for me.

I return Claudia's call and the news is good. Later, over salad, I tell Bunny that Claudia has gotten a writing assignment from Jesse Simmons for his new series. It will also serve as a tryout for a staff position which means a weekly paycheck and stability. Bunny nods and smiles sweetly and asks me at least twice just how Claudia Hicks has become a part of our lives. I tell my loving wife that I will let her know as soon as I can but for the moment, mum's the word and I'm not talking about French champagne.

Friday morning. Bertha is going in for her procedure which, I have been told, is not lengthy. I'm up earlier than usual because I am set to drive her to her eye doctor's office even though she tried to tell me it was unnecessary. A cab will do just fine and her nurse will be constantly at her side. Maybe so but I vetoed the cab whether she liked it or not. The nurse she can keep and after I have dropped her off I will spend the rest of Friday riding herd on the office gang, not that they need it, but I promised as part of our pact that I would crack the whip and restore a sense of order to our brilliant but undisciplined staff.

I park in front of her house and start up the walk just as the door opens and she emerges with a woman in white at her side. Seeing me Bertha speeds up a little, shouting as she nears me.

"What in God's name are you up to?" she asks.

"Up to how? What are you talking about?" I ask.

"This man Haller called me first thing this morning. I wasn't even out of bed yet and he's calling you all sorts of a fool and me for putting up with you."

"Ignore the bastard," I say.

"Isn't he the man who puts out that dreadful gossip magazine?"

"Yes, and ignore him anyway. I'm dealing with him. You have enough on your mind."

"Yes, but—"

"No buts, Bert. Everything's under control." I check out the nurse. "And you are?"

"Mady Riordon, Mr. Bernardi," she says. Brunette, blue eyes, fortyish and built like a pro wrestler.

"You've been warned about Miss Bowles pigheadedness?"

"I have and we have no problems, the lady and myself. We're going to have a grand old time."

"Good luck," I mutter under my breath and then we get Bert into my car and take off. At Bert's insistence I leave them off at the doctor's doorstep. I watch as she and Mady walk to the front door and go inside, then I'm back in the car and off to the office where I will play CEO for one day. I'm not sure how my day will lay out but I know for sure where my first phone call will be directed.

"Hollywood Exposed." says a bored female voice. Sparkling, vivacious Gladys Primm

"This is Joseph Bernardi. Put Mr. Haller on the phone."

"I'm sorry, sir, but Mr. Haller is away from the office this morning."

"Are you sure? Why don't you look in his bathroom and see if he's hiding in the commode?"

"Sir?"

"When do you expect him, Miss Primm?"

"I don't know, sir. If you'd like to leave your name and phone—"

"I would not," I say. "I'll call again later."

I slam down the phone. As Joe Louis, the champ, once sagely said about his upcoming bout with the lighter but faster Billy Conn, 'He can run but he can't hide.' Ditto for Nate Haller.

I reach in my wallet and extract a small piece of paper on which I have written Brett Klinger's phone number. It's eight-thirty-five. He should be up and about by now. If not, he will be.

"Hello," he says after nine rings. His voice is heavy and slurry. I've awakened him. Either that or he has a serious drinking problem.

"Brett? Hi. Joe Bernardi. Hope I didn't wake you." I'm casual and breezy, an old pal reconnecting.

Silence. Then, "Joe who?"

"Joe Bernardi. Bowles & Bernardi. You came to us a couple of years ago with that terrific screenplay, the one about Teddy Roosevelt being lost in the Black Hills with amnesia and Sitting Bull rescuing him from Cochise and the Apaches."

"Oh, yeah, yeah," he says with zero certainty. "Yeah, Joe Bernardi. Sure, how are you, Joe? Been a while."

"Sure has," I say. I can hear a woman's voice in the background and Klinger's trying to shut her up. "Who's that, Brett? Is that Violet? Smart lady. I remember her well."

"Broke up."

"What?"

"I said, me and Violet broke up. A long story."

"Oh, too bad. Say, I read that piece you did on Greg Lunsford.

First rate."

"Thanks."

"Fascinating guy."

"If you say so. Tell me again, Joe, why you're calling."

"Something's come up. I think you and I can do a little business together."

"Concerning?"

"Lunsford and Nathan Haller. Are you free later this afternoon? There's a few bucks in it for you."

"Sure. Sounds good.Uh—Joe—"

"What?"

"Are you still in the business? I thought I heard otherwise."

"You heard wrong, Brett. How about my office at three-thirty?"

"Okay."

"You know where it is?"

"I've been there."

"See you at three-thirty then."

I hang up. Bertha. Brett. Two down, one to go.

I call Universal and ask for Eddie Dodds, the *Columbo* unit manager. Dodds isn't at his desk but his assistant tells me that Falk will be shooting the rest of the morning on the back lot. She says she will arrange for a drive-on pass. I thank her and hang up. Before I leave I summon Mallory Evans who assures me that everything is running smoothly and that none of my proteges is acting like a prima donna, at least not so far. I tell Mallory to spread the word that I should be back right after lunch and also that the company payroll is running in the red to the tune of one salary and to reassure them all that I will not act precipitously to solve the problem before five o'clock this afternoon unless forced to do so. Mallory smiles. She gets it. Nothing like a little self-interest to keep the machinery meshing smoothly.

I'm able to find a spot near Stage 15. There's a lot of activity in this sector and it's only when I spot the camera that I realize that this isn't normal studio traffic, this is the scene that's about to be shot. The psychiatrist's mistress, Joan Hudson, played by Katherine Justice, is a bit player in a movie and Columbo has caught up with her at work to ask 'one or two simple questions'. Now I also spot Peter and the director Dick Irving, their heads together by the entrance to Stage 16. A pretty girl in a pink hoochy-coochy outfit is also a part of the conversation. Miss Justice, no doubt. I edge closer but do not interrupt. It's only when the gathering breaks up that I approach Peter. He beams when he sees me coming.

"What are you doing here, babysitting?" he asks.

"Watching out for the merchandise," I say.

"Great. I've graduated from being the next Julie Garfield to merchandise."

To the New York theater crowd John Garfield was always known as Julie and probably will be for years to come.

"If you wanted respect, you should have become a cantor," I say.

"You haven't heard me sing," he replies lighting up a nearly new cigar.

"We need to talk," I say.

"Good. So talk."

"Over lunch."

"Okay, in my dressing room. I made myself a tomato and relish sandwich on rye. I don't know what time we break. Wait a second." He looks around, then shouts at one of the grips. "Hey, Manny! When do we break for lunch?"

"How the hell should I know?" comes the shouted reply.

Peter shakes his head.

"How do you like that guy? They tell me the crew guys know everything about what's going on, I gotta shout at the one guy who doesn't know what day it is."

"Why don't I meet you at your dressing room? I'll have the

commissary send around a burger and fries."

"Sounds like a plan," Peter says. "Tell 'em to make it two."

"Two what?"

"Two burgers, two fries. One for me, one for you."

"What about your tomato and relish sandwich?"

"Oh, I hate tomato and relish but there was nothing else in the refrigerator."

"I see."

"Anyway I think there was something wrong with the tomato. Half of it is firm, the other half is soft and goopy. You know what I mean by goopy?"

"Sure," I say.

"Hard to understand," he says with a puzzled look on his face. "It looked okay when I bought it at the beginning of last week."

I nod, waiting for him to start on the shortcomings of the bread and relish but he doesn't and forty minutes later we're seated at the table in his dressing room, scarfing down the burgers.

"I saw the dailies from yesterday. They're good, Pete. Very good."

"Yeah, I saw 'em first thing this morning with Dick and the camera guys. Not half bad."

"You seem to have the character nailed pretty good," I say.

"That? That stuff? That's just the beginning. Wait'll I really get going."

A big dollop of ketchup falls on his raincoat as he takes a bite of his burger. He wipes it away with the sleeve of his raincoat, then dips his napkin in his water glass and wipes the sleeve clean.

"I'm a very messy eater," he tells me. "Can't tell you why, I just am. You know, Joe, there's a lot of me in this Columbo guy. Maybe you noticed."

"I noticed," I say. "Look, Peter, the guys at the network, they love what they're seeing and they want to up the ante."

"What's that supposed to mean?"

"It means they're willing to commit to thirteen episodes to start airing next September."

"A series?" His expression darkens. "Come on, Joe, we talked about this. I did a series, remember? The hours were lousy, we never got the scripts on time, we'd get behind and have to work weekends—No, I don't think so."

"I know what they're prepared to offer, Pete. We're talking millions here, Pete, not bad for a kid from Ossining, New York."

"Yeah and the grind'll kill me before I get a chance to spend it. Tell 'em no, Joe. Not interested."

"You get director approval, script approval, even cast approval. Ray Burr would kill for a deal like that."

"Fine," Peter says. "Tell Ray Burr to get his big butt out of that wheelchair and come over here and play Columbo and I'll go back to New York where I belong."

"I'm only saying—"

"I hear what you're saying, Joe," Peter says, raising his voice, "and the answer is no. It was no a month ago and it'll be no in the future and I would appreciate it if you would respect my wishes so I do not have to raise my voice which I do not like to do, especially to a good friend like you."

"No series," I say.

"That's right. No series, no way, no how."

"No way. No how," I repeat.

Peter grins.

"Now you're talking," he says.

I grin back. Now all I have to do is explain this to Sid Sheinberg.

We finish lunching chatting about everything but the film and what may or may not come next. Peter regales me with stories of working off-off Broadway and his experiences with Jason Robards on 'The Iceman Cometh'. Little theater in New York City is not for the faint of heart but for those who prevail the rewards are often great. Peter is good and he knows it but he also knows he's been lucky and for that he is grateful. He has a charisma that others would kill for and I hope he never loses it.

Quarter to two. His phone rings. He's needed on the set for a run through with Katherine Justice. We exit his dressing room and he heads toward Stage 15, me in the direction of the Black Tower and the Bank of America. The last time I opened my wallet I found myself staring at a fiver and two wrinkled ones. Time to restock the treasury.

As I approach the doors to the bank I look to my right where I spot them. Bart Kane is leaning up against the building smoking a cigarette and the hatchet-faced secretary, Gladys Primm, is irritably checking and re-checking her wrist watch. For a moment, I freeze in place then quickly pass them by. Bart Kane is looking in a different direction and doesn't see me but I lock stares with Primm and her expression is icy. However I know one thing: where Nate Haller goes, Bart Kane goes so there's no question Haller is in the building. But where? In the bank or on one of the upper floors, pumping some poor underpaid secretary for dirt on one of Universal's many television stars? Which?

It's the bank and the moment I walk in I spot him.

CHAPTER EIGHT

I am sitting down, pressed up against the wall at the head of the staircase that leads fourteen stories straight down to the lobby. It is dim, very dim, with one low wattage light bulb over the door and ambient light coming from the nearby elevator shafts. There are six of them. None of the elevators are operational, the building-wide lockdown took care of that, and the cabs are motionless, all trapped at various floors or between them, some with passengers, and some without. When the lockdown switch is thrown, everything paralyzes. Elevators freeze no matter their location and all exterior doors to the building automatically lock. If a bank robber has been trapped within the Tower's walls, he will be apprehended. There is no avenue of escape. The same would apply to an innocent bystander who foolishly looked over the roof ledge to the crowd below and found his photo being taken by a tourist from some hick town east of San Bernardino.

The walls are thick, the door is steel and sturdy and yet I can still hear noise coming from outside. It is the sound of the police helicopter hovering over the roof. An officer is down, having fallen from a height of at least twelve feet. The chopper had been ready to touch down when it suddenly lurched and the shooter lost his grip and fell. The question is, what is the chopper pilot going to do about it. The injured officer was the designated shooter. Is there a back up on board? Is the pilot still going to land? Or is the pilot going to fly away to pick up backup and maybe a medic to treat the injured officer.

Unwittingly I have stumbled into a dangerous situation. At least twice in the past four days I have made very public threats against Nathan Haller and now he is lying fourteen stories away, his blood soaked body splayed in a hideous position while strangers gawk. Did he accidentally fall from the roof, did he jump, or was he pushed? Honestly I favor option three. Haller was too much in love with himself to self-destruct. And here I am, hiding high atop the Black Tower only moments after Haller died from his fall and most rational people will conclude that I might have had something to do with it. Like a powerful shove in the back, perhaps. Can I blame them?

But I know something that the ground level mob doesn't know. I'm talking about that quick flash of grey flannel that disappeared into the doorway just as the door was closing. I know that someone was on the roof with Haller before I showed up. I strongly suspect that someone to be Greg Lunsford even though Lunsford was still in the lobby when I started to climb the stairs in pursuit of Haller. Could he have passed me by? Yes, it could have happened when I left the stairwell to query the mailroom kid on the eleventh floor. Is this farfetched? Yes. Am I that desperate for an explanation? Perhaps so but three things are undeniable. Haller is dead, I saw something or someone in the doorway just before the door closed, and in the absence of any other logical and provable explanation, the police are going to be coming after me on a charge of first degree murder.

Suddenly I am aware that the noise from the chopper's rotator blades is louder but steady. With the door partly open I take another cautious look. The chopper has settled and the pilot, who I now recognize as being female, is out of the cab and has gone to the aid of the shooter who is lying injured on the roof. She tries to help him to his feet but it's impossible. He's too big, she's too slight. The shooter needs a medic and the pilot needs a shooter, perhaps even more than one, to complete her mission. She makes sure the man is lying comfortably and then she dashes back to the cockpit and a moment later the chopper is lifting off. I open the door wider for a better look at the chopper as it heads west toward Valley Division headquarters. As I do I glance at the injured shooter and find him staring at me. Quickly I shut the door. How good a look did he get? I have no idea.

Now it is quiet and I know I must move. Unquestionably the appearance of the pilot is being mirrored below by the participation of LAPD officers, perhaps even some of Jake McElrath's studio security force. They will slowly work their way up, floor by floor, and the shooter or shooters who return with the pilot will start working their way down, meticulously searching every floor for either a non-existent bank robber or, far more likely, the person or persons responsible for Nate Haller's demise. I am sure of one thing. I cannot be caught 'hiding'. I've got to find people and blend in. Fortunately I am well enough known by the Universal executives that mixing in will not present a problem and absent a reliable eyewitness and if I am very very lucky, I can successfully hide in plain sight.

Cautiously I stand, my back still pressed against the wall. My 48 year old body has become less and less tolerant of physical exertion these days and tells me so in a hundred different ways, mostly aches and pains but sometimes with lightheadedness or dizziness. I stretch and shake my head vigorously. No problems, I'm okay. I grab the railing and start down the steps to the 14th Floor landing. I decide right away that I will bypass this floor. I know most of these executives and Lew Wasserman and I are on a first name basis, but 14 is less densely populated than 12 and I need lots of people around to get lost in. 12 is headquarters for the TV people and I have legitimate business to discuss with them. My presence will not be questioned.

As soon as I leave the 12th floor stairwell and step into the corridor, it hits me. Normally hushed and sedate the entire floor is abuzz with activity. Secretaries are on their phones either talking to family or placing calls for their bosses. The few phones not in use for outgoing are ringing persistently. The word is already out. I spot a small screen TV on a secretarial desk. It's tuned to Channel 4 and a talking head is describing the events at Universal City. He is sharing screen time with an on-site reporter who is standing in the middle of Lankershim Boulevard, the Tower in the background. I have no idea what he's saying - the volume is muted- but I suspect the situation is being described in breathless terms usually associated with reports of alien invaders.

I pass by the open door to Sid Sheinberg's office and spot a couple of writers sitting patiently, waiting for Sheinberg to rejoin them. Sid is standing at his secretary's desk with phone in hand explaining to his wife Lorraine that no one is in danger and that the lockdown is merely a precaution. At the far end of the hallway, Frank Price and Robert Harris are looking out the huge picture window, staring down at the gathering crowd jamming the studio entrance. I join them as two more LAPD cruisers pull up outside the front gate and park on Lankershim which appears to have been blocked off to traffic in both directions.

I have been keeping my eye out for some sign of Greg Lunsford but so far no luck. I ask Frank if he's seen him this morning. He says no. Harris chimes in. He, too, has seen nothing of Lunsford. Maybe not but I know he's here in the building somewhere. He has to be and sooner or later he will show.

I walk away from the window and go in search of Charlie Engel. Maybe Charlie's spotted him. It would makes sense. Charlie's the exec who oversees two of Lunsford's three shows. I'm wrong. Charlie's in his office but he's alone, watching the news reports on television. When he sees me standing in the doorway, he waves me in.

"The world's gone nuts," he says.

"Amen to that," I echo.

"Nate Haller. What was he doing on our roof?" he asks.

"Maybe he got a tip that Hitchcock was up there doing the nasty with his latest blonde star."

"Don't be cynical, Joe," Charlie says eyes fixed on his television set. Suddenly he leans forward as then face of a slim young man wearing a Lakers cap fills the screen. "This is the guy with the camera," Charlie says.

"Who?"

"Some tourist here sightseeing. He managed to take a picture of the guy who pushed Haller off the roof."

"You're kidding," I say. "Actually caught it on film?"

"Not exactly," Charlie says. "Maybe a half a minute after Haller goes splat on the pavement, this man comes peeking over the edge off the roof. Probably wanted to make sure Haller was dead."

"Like the old guy was going to survive fourteen stories?" I scoff.

"Probably too far away for a decent picture but the police sent the film over to the Technicolor lab next door for developing. The guy's camera was a top of the line Argus 35mm and he told the cops he was pretty sure he got a good enough shot that it'll show something, even if they have to enlarge it a couple of times."

I remember him. That damned tourist, his camera aimed skyward. No flash but the morning sky was bright. No, I think, to myself. Don't panic. Fourteen stories. At least a hundred and fifty feet away. There's no possibility. No camera is that good.

The tourist is talking to the on-site reporter.

"Harvey Dowd. I'm from Azusa and no, I'm not a professional.

I shoot birds a lot and also when I go to some kind of event where I might run into a celebrity, I like to have it with me. Opening day at Dodger Stadium I got a shot of Lee Marvin. I wasn't very close but I got him. He was eating a hot dog."

Harvey Dowd from Azusa is a nebbishy kind of guy and that has me worried because he's nebbishy enough to be correct about how good his camera is.

"Any idea how long we'll be here?" I ask.

Charlie shakes his head.

"I called Jeannie few minutes ago and told her not to expect me any time soon. Jake McElrath, the security guy, was on camera a while ago and said he had six witnesses from the bank who saw this guy chasing Haller into the stairwell, yelling threats. Sounds like they're going to start letting people out, one at a time, through the bank entrance with the witnesses ready to identify the man when he tries to leave."

My heart sinks. They'll descend on me like a swarm of locusts. My chances of getting out of this have just sunk from slim to not-on-your-life.

The broadcast has just returned from a commercial for a local dentist to find the reporter joined on camera by studio security chief, Jake McElrath.

"And we're back," the reporter says, "and once again I am joined by Jacob McElrath, head of security for Universal Studios."

"That's Jake," McElrath says.

"What?"

"It's Jake. Not Jacob. Just Jake."

"Okay, I understand. Well, Jake or Jacob has just informed me that there seems to be a problem with the bank's security cameras. Could you explain that to us, Mr. McElrath?"

"That's Lieutenant," McElrath says. "Not Mister. I command a cadre of seven, a sergeant and six officers."

"My mistake, Lieutenant," the reporter says, squirming slightly. "Could you tell us about the cameras?"

"Sure. The tapes are useless. One camera malfunctioned and the other two were not positioned to capture the suspect's face. We got a fleeting glance as he ran past the camera toward the staircase doorway but it didn't tell us much. The man had dark hair and was wearing a dark colored suit, could have been navy blue or charcoal grey."

"That's all you were able to get?"

"I'd say he's five eleven, maybe a little taller but that's just a guess."

"And what do your witnesses say?"

"You don't want to know," McElrath says in disgust.

"Actually, yes, I do want to know," says the reporter testily.

"Well, one woman said the man was at least sixty years old and his hair was turning white. Another said he was no taller than five-nine because that's how tall her late husband was. An older gentleman said he looked a lot like Ricardo Cortez, an old movie actor, while his companion said, no, he looked a lot more like Warren William, another has-been. One dead, one not. A fifth witness said he was sure the man had a pronounced limp, probably a shortened right leg but he wasn't sure about that, and the last eyewitness saw a handlebar mustache that no one else seemed to notice. All six swear they will know the man on sight the instant they see him. So much for eyewitness testimony."

Rap, rap.

A knock on the doorjamb. I look up to see Sid Sheinberg framed in the doorway.

"I thought I caught a glimpse of you earlier, Joe. Got a minute?" he smiles.

I get to my feet.

"For you, Sid, minutes galore."

"Any word, Sid, about how long this is going to keep up?"

Charlie asks.

"I know what you know, Charlie, and it isn't much. Come on, Joe, I have a couple of guys I want you to meet."

I go to the door, giving Charlie a little thumbs up, and follow Sid down the corridor to his office. Everywhere I hear the low volume television reportage of the Tower lockdown. Just before I enter, I look down the cross corridor and there is Greg Lunsford, a smile on his face, drink in hand, leaning against the wall and staring lasciviously down at one of Universal's newly hired female executives. I forget her name. Lucy. Lily. She's newly married with a big rock on her finger. Did I mention that young newlyweds were second only to interns on Lunsford's to-do list? However I'm most startled, not by his behavior, but by his appearance. Usually the epitome of a well dressed writer-producer, Lunsford's collar is uncharacteristically open, his tie yanked down and his jacket shows faint signs of smudges. Odd. Very odd, I think, as Sid leads me into his office to introduce me to the pair from whose fertile brains the character of Columbo had emerged several years ago.

They stand as Sid handles the introductions. Levinson is a forty year old beanpole with a balding pate. His partner, Link, is short, also follicle-challenged and wears a wisp of a goatee to make up for it. If Mutt and Jeff had not already been created by Bud Fisher these two would make ideal models. I have heard they have been friends from their pre-teen years and have been writing together since junior high school. If and when they start finishing each other's sentences, I will know I have not been misled.

"I thought it time for you fellows to meet since Dick and Bill will be producing Columbo when it goes to series," Sid says.

I am about to blurt out 'Wait a minute' when Levinson beats me to it.

"Wait a minute, Sid. Bill and I haven't committed to any series and you know it."

Sid smiles. "A matter of time, Dick. You've seen the dailies, The guy has star written all over him.The public's gonna lap this up like iced tea."

I'm not sure iced tea is something you lap up but Levinson plows right ahead anyway.

"Well, the public can lap it up without us. Look, Sid, I like Peter. He's a terrific guy but he's also an actor and worse than that, a perfectionist actor. He wants everything as perfect as possible. If he'd been producing 'Gone With the Wind', the editor would still be working on the final cut."

"You're exaggerating," Sid says.

"Am I? Ask the people involved with 'The Trials of O'Brien'. A terrific show. Peter was terrific. The rest of it? A nightmare. Not everybody felt that way but enough. Actors act, producers produce. Peter doesn't seem to grasp that."

"You're going on hearsay, Dick—"

"Not so. Yesterday evening he was in the editorial room with Dick Wray helping him cut a scene together."

Sid shakes his head.

"Naturally as an actor he wanted to protect his performance—"

"He wasn't even in the scene!!" Levinson says, raising his decibel count by at least 50.

Sid stares at him, finally at a loss for words.

I feel I am now obligated to clear the air.

"Uh, excuse me—"

"Life's too short, Sid," Levinson says.

"Dick's right," Link chimes in. "We've got movies we want to make. We haven't the time or the patience to baby-sit a --a—"

"Broadway prima donna," Dick says, finishing his partner's sentence. Now I'm sold. Here sit Rodgers and Hammerstein, Gilbert and Sullivan and Kaufman and Hart.

"Excuse me—" I start to try again.

"You're not giving him a chance," Sid complains.

"Neither will the director when Falk starts giving the other actors line readings," Levinson says.

"Excuse me!!!" I bark it out so loudly that I scare myself. All eyes turn in my direction. "I hate to throw cold water on this spirited discussion but I feel obligated to tell you that Peter has no interest in doing a *Columbo* series. Not now and not ever and knowing him as I do, when he digs in his heels, the time for discussion is over."

CHAPTER NINE

From the expressions on their faces you'd have thought I'd passed gas in a crude and noisy fashion but of course, I had not. I had just brought the three of them face to face with reality. Like it or not, Peter Falk is his own man and though he is far from rich, his innate good sense, which features no dollar signs on his belief system, is saying TV movie, yes, TV series no.

"You're not mistaken?" Sheinberg asks.

"I am not."

"If this is a ploy to get more money—" Sheinberg continues.

"It isn't. He knows how much is on the table and he agrees it's a fair amount. That isn't the issue, the issue is the pressures of a weekly television series, the half-baked scripts, often mediocre casts, by-the-numbers directors who are little more than traffic cops because there's never enough time. A series is a series is a series and Peter wants no part of it."

"NBC is crazy about the dailies," Sheinberg says. "They think the series is a foregone conclusion. So did I until just now." He scratches his head and sits down behind his desk. He looks around at the three of us. "So what now, gentlemen?"

"We could always recast with someone willing to do the series," Link says with a straight face. "I hear Lawrence Tierney's available."

It's the first I've seen of Link's quiet, pixie-like sense of humor. Tierney's claim to fame is playing the title role in the 1945 gangster flick, 'Dillinger' and little else of note.

"Get serious, Bill," Sheinberg says.

"Okay, then how about Sonny Tufts?" Still deadpan. Tufts was a leading man of limited abilities who prospered during the war years when the elite of the industry's leading men were fighting the war.

Sheinberg fixes Link with a jaundiced stare.

"Thank you, Bill, for your efforts to make sure this property never goes to series but we are not going to recast. We are going to make 'Prescription: Murder' with Peter Falk and worry about the series later."

"And what are you going to tell NBC?" Levinson asks.

"That any talk of a series is premature, that Falk is settling into the role but doesn't want to be pressured and that you two fellas are loaded down with movie of the week commitments which you're not sure you want to scuttle for an exacting show which could go belly up after a mere 13 episodes."

Levinson looks at him suspiciously.

"Sid, if I didn't know you better, that sounds a lot like a ploy to get the network to raise the commitment to 22 episodes and to pony up a lot bigger licensing fee."

Sheinberg smiles. "Dick, would I do a thing like that?"

Dick smiles back. "Does Little Miss Muffet sit on a tuffet?"

The phone rings on Sheinberg's desk. In a moment a buzz and his secretary's voice. "McElrath," she says over the intercom. Sheinberg picks up.

"Yes, Jake. Yes, we've been watching"

"Uh-huh."

"Twenty minutes."

"Who?"

"Don't know her."

"When?"

"Right away"

"Okay, I'll pass the word."

"And Jake? What about those strange faces? Is that going any-where?"

"Right...Stay in touch." He hangs up and then steps out of his office and speaks quietly to his secretary at her desk just outside his door. She hurries off and Sheinberg steps back into the office.

"They expect to have that photo developed momentarily," Sheinberg says. "When they do, they'll start letting people out of the building one at a time through a door in the bank lobby with witnesses looking on."

"But still no idea who they're after," I venture cautiously.

"None. Meanwhile the secretary can't remember his name but she is positive she'll know him on sight."

"Secretary? What secretary?" Levinson asks.

"Haller's secretary. She says yesterday this man came to Haller's office and threatened his life. Today she saw the same man enter the bank less than a minute before the alarm sounded and the building was locked down."

"No name?" I ask.

"She doesn't remember it because the man didn't have an appoint-ment. Anyway they're activating one of the elevators and taking her up to the roof and a SWAT team is going to bring her down, floor by floor, trying to find and identify this man. Jake McElrath says it'll be a pretty thorough search starting about fifteen minutes from now. We're spreading the word throughout the floors."

My collar has suddenly gotten very tight. No question that the hatchet faced Miss Primm will scream bloody murder the moment she sees my face.

"Also, and this is important," Sheinberg continues, "we were asked to identify any strangers wandering around our corridors.

There are none on this floor, gentlemen, at least none we can find, and Jake says he's getting the same report from all the floors."

"So the idea of a bank robber—"Levinson starts to say.

"There was no attempted robbery, just a teller with a twitchy finger on the alarm button," Sheinberg says. "No, they're looking for the man who may have shoved Nathan Haller off the roof and it looks as if that person is either someone who works here or someone with whom our people work."

"Either way I think we should pin a medal on him," Link suggests.

"I agree," I say. "I also think it's very likely that the guy is about to be immortalized on 'Los Angeles Badges". I can see Greg Lunsford now, calling his story editor and ordering up a script for two weeks from now, a true life story, ripped from the headlines. Showbiz Sleazebag Splattered on Studio Sidewalk by Widowed Wife of Unjustly Accused Co—Fireman—you fill in the blank! The usual Lunsford crap, phony sentimentality and plenty of violence. Sorry, I mean to say 'action'. The network doesn't do violence, just two fist fights, three car chases, a half dozen babes walking around nearly bare-assed and a humorous tag at the end to lighten things up. Ho ho ho. Go to commercial. Like I said, the usual Lunsford crap."

I'm not sure why I blurted out all of that. Maybe I just wanted to make sure Lunsford was placed in the middle of this maelstrom. Or maybe I just wanted to vent my spleen over the huge bucks being made by a man of so little talent and apparently even less integrity.

"A lot of people like that usual crap, Joe," Sheinberg says to me.

"And a lot of people also believe in horoscopes, seances, and professional wrestling. But I wouldn't want them on my jury if I were being tried for murder."

I look up as Greg Lunsford's frame suddenly fills the doorway.

"Am I interrupting this convention or can anyone join in," he asks with a smile.

"We were just talking about you, Greg," I say pleasantly.

"Come in and grab a chair, Greg," Sheinberg says, cutting me off before I can continue my diatribe. Lunsford looks just as disheveled as he did a few minutes ago leering all over the cute new addition to the executive corps. His suit is still rumpled and his face is smudged and sweaty and now, for the first time, I notice that the Phi Beta Kappa key which he so vainly displays on a gold chain across his middle is missing.

"Can't stay, Sid," Lunsford says. "Just looking for an update on when we can blow this fire trap?" He grins at his pale imitation of wit.

"Soon, I'm told," Sheinberg says. "You can always take the stairs to the lobby, Greg, be one of the first ones out."

"Thanks, I'll wait for the elevators," Lunsford says. He starts to turn away. My voice stops him.

"Looks like you were in quite a brawl, Greg," I say, gesturing toward his suit.

"This? No. I fell asleep in one of your conference rooms. Suit just needs a good pressing." Another phony smile to go with a lame lie and then he's gone.

I get to my feet.

"Excuse me, fellas," I say, "but my bladder's just been put me on tinkle alert. Be right back."

I exit the room, spot Lunsford and hurry after him. When I reach him we are outside an empty conference room. I grab him hard by the elbow and steer him, startled, through the open doorway. His frame is big but his body is soft. He isn't hard to control.

"What the hell are you doing, Bernardi?" he says angrily, shrugging me off of him.

"You're not going to get away with it, Lunsford."

"What are you talking about?"

"You were seen, I know you were. You had to have been seen. Too many people like to hang around up top, to enjoy some fresh air and get away from the phones, that kind of thing. Me, I just saw you leaving by the doorway but somebody saw you actually shove the old guy, no question about that and whoever it is they're going to speak up. Maybe not today, maybe not tomorrow but someday soon"

"You're crazy!" he growls.

He pushes past me and starts for the door.

"That wrinkled suit didn't come from any nap," I shout after him. "Haller put up a fight."

He whirls back at me.

"And maybe you'd like to tell the cops what YOU were doing up there. I'm not the guy who threatened to kill him, Bernardi, you are and not just once. What? Nothing to say? Quiet for a change? Next time, think before you open your mouth, Bernardi, or you'll be the one wearing steel bracelets."

"Well, you keep repeating your fairy tale, Lunsford. Maybe if you tell it enough times, you'll begin to believe it yourself. As for me, I'm not worried. I'm not the guy who's going to get the phone call in the middle of the night and some guy with a muffled voice saying I know what you did, I saw you and I want money, lots of it. You know how that works, don't you, Lunsford? Like when Nate Haller called asking for money only once wasn't enough for greedy old Nate so he called again and you knew there'd never be an end to it so you did the only thing you could. Am I close? Is that how it was?"

If he's afraid he doesn't show it. He glares at me and there is nothing in his eyes but hate.

"Watch your back, Bernardi." he says softly. "I'm warning you. Max Mannix is my number two guy and he handles problems I can't handle myself. And if you don't know who Max is, ask around."

Then he's gone and I don't follow him. How can I? He's right. I can't really swear he was on that roof although we both know he was. And if I did swear, where does that leave me? On the roof with Lunsford and the two of us playing He Said, He Said. As for Max Mannix I know who he is and he scares the hell out of me but scared or not, I've got to come up with some way to pin the tail on this particular donkey.

I leave the conference room and look up and down the corridor. Lunsford's made himself scarce. I head back in the direction of Charlie Engel's office. The TV set is still on and Charlie is at a bookshelf fixing a cup of tea from a two-unit hot plate.

"Hey, Joe, how about a cup of tea?"

"No. No thanks, Charlie. I just dropped in for an update. Anything new?" I ask positioning myself in front of the TV set.

"Nope. Last I heard they were about to put that photograph on the screen, you know, the one of the guy looking down from the roof though what it means, I'll be damned if I know. Ten to one it's just some curious mail room guy up there making out with his girlfriend."

"Yeah. Love. Ain't it grand?" I say mirthlessly.

"So, I hear you just tore Greg Lunsford a new one, Joe," Charlie says offhandedly.

"Where'd you hear that?"

"One of the secretaries passing by an open doorway."

"I've got no use for the guy," I say. "Can't help it."

"Not one of my favorite people either, Joe, but I've got to work with him. I guess you've heard the latest."

"About Lunsford? No. What?"

"He'd been banging this cute little extra, Mitzi something. Mitzi Moore, I think. You know the type, a bright-eyed Nebraska farm girl looking for a break. Finally Greg got tired of her and sent her back to her husband. Three nights ago she offed herself. She was two months pregnant. Times had the story on Page 21. Lunsford wasn't mentioned by name but everybody knows it's him. Miserable prick lives a charmed life."

"Not only that, he's got Max Mannix," I say in disgust.

The on-site news reporter comes back on screen from commercial next to a scrawny guy sporting a weird blonde mohawk and wearing an aqua blue silk shirt.

"I'm here with Mr. Wesley Prince who has just been released from the casting offices located in the lower level of the Universal Black Tower. Can you tell me, Mr. Prince, how long you were detained by the authorities before they let you go?"

"Well, I can tell you it was only slightly shorter than the last ice age." he says, very pouty. "Two cupcakes and a bottle of water, that was my entire lunch, if you can imagine such a thing."

"You are an actor?"

"I am and I had a very important interview with Mr. Geoffrey Fischer who is one of their excellent casting directors, the very best, sweetheart, and I was in the middle of reading for the part of this sexually liberated librarian when pandemonium broke out, all sorts of bells and whistles, I thought for a moment I was a passenger on the Titanic, it was that chilling. I'd say this was about ten minutes to two. I know because my appointment was one-thirty and I'd taken a few minutes to become conversant with my sides"

The reporter turns his head, distracted by someone who has come up next to him and handed him something surreptitiously. The cameraman edits Wesley Prince from the frame and concentrates on the newcomer who is introduced as a technician with the technicolor lab.

"I must apologize for the quality of the print," the technicolor guy is saying, "but it's the best we could do on short notice."

"I'm sure it's fine," the TV reporter is saying. "Let's have a look."

He takes the photo from the technicolor guy and peers at it closely. "Better than nothing," he says, holding the snap in front of the camera as I suck in my breath nervously.

It's a photo of a guy, that much is certain, but the image is blurred and a shadow has fallen across the left side of his face. It could easily be LBJ or Dick Nixon or even Joe DiMaggio but when television news gets a shootable prop or clue, it uses it no matter how useless it really is. I exhale, relieved.

"I got it," Charlie says looking over my shoulder. "No question who it is." I look back at him. "Quasimodo," he says. "Don't you remember, Laughton peering down from the bell tower of Notre Dame at the crowd milling below screaming 'Sanctuary! Sanctuary!'"

I laugh, humoring him, but a second look only leads to a feeling of relief. The blurred image, the dark shadow, this is one unpleasant looking guy and he doesn't look a thing like me. I am less worried now about the witnesses in the bank lobby who can't seem to agree on much and this photo isn't going to resolve matters. The real danger will be coming from above in the form of Haller's secretary. I'm getting squeezed between a rock and a hard place and I need help. I turn to Charlie.

"Mind if I use your phone?" I ask.

"Help yourself," he says, concentrating on the television screen.

I dial the office and after a few moments, Glenda Mae comes on the line.

"It's me," I say.

"I was wondering when you'd get back to me."

"Been busy. Long story. What have you got for me on Lunsford?"

"Not much you don't already know. Meanwhile I've got a guy here says he had a three-thirty with you. Brett Klinger. Ring a bell?"

I look at my watch. It's ten minutes to four. Shit.

"Put him on," I say.

"You're welcome," she says pointedly.

"Please," I say.

"That's better," she says, "Please hold for Mr. Klinger."

A few moments of silence, then:

"Bernardi?"

"Sorry, Brett. I was unavoidably detained, as they say. In fact I still am. I'm in the Black Tower."

"Then you must be having an adventuresome afternoon."

"You might say that. Look, what I need to know is—"

Klinger interrupts me.

"What you need to know is something we'll discuss face to face, Bernardi," he says, "and when you mentioned there were a few bucks involved, I'm afraid it's going to be more than just a few."

"I can't get out of here just now—"

"That's your problem," Klinger says. "Not mine."

I mull my options. They aren't good. He has something damaging he wants to sell or he wouldn't have showed up at the office.

"I'll meet you for dinner at Chasen's at six o'clock," I say.

"And if you're not out of there by then?"

"I will be, one way or another," I tell him.

"Big talk."

"There's a C note in it for you whether I show or not. Order dinner and sign my name to the check. I'll phone Dave Chasen and authorize it. If I'm not there by the time you finish desert, we'll try to connect tomorrow."

"I'm partial to Maine lobster," Klinger says.

"Go nuts," I reply. "Put my girl back on the phone."

I ask Glenda Mae to call Dave Chasen and guarantee Klinger's dinner tab which she happily says she will do. Only when I tell her that I am fine and in no danger does she hang up. Gotta love her. Loyal to a fault.

One more phone call to go. I need to know what, if anything, Mick's boys were able to dig up on Nathan Haller. But just then, the camera at the base of the Tower swings up and zooms in on the roof as a man in civvies appears and gives the high sign. A female stands at his side, Haller's secretary no doubt, too blurry to tell.

There's also something vaguely familiar about the man. They'll be entering the building any moment now, first checking the fourteenth floor and then appearing here on the twelfth. I need to descend lower into the building if I am going to have any time at all to talk with Mick who is digging into Nate Haller's past. With Haller dead, anything Mick has been able to discover will probably be moot but you never know.

I turn my attention back to Charlie Engel.

"Charlie, is there anything in this building like a library, you know, some place where they'd have back issues of the trades and maybe some books?"

He frowns, thinking.

"Oliver Kemp, maybe. I know he keeps current with the movie mags. Also keeps a lot of star bios on hand to settle bar bets. You might try him."

"Where do I find this guy?"

"Fifth floor. He's one of the corporate lawyers. Nice enough but kind of squirrely."

"Oliver Kemp," I say.

"Oliver Kemp," he replies.

I start for the door, then turn back.

"Charlie, in case anybody asks, you haven't seen me and in particular, you have no idea where I went."

"Not a clue," he says with a reassuring smile and I'm out of there.

CHAPTER TEN

I duck into the stairwell and start down. I can hear voices coming from above. One belongs to a woman and I'm pretty sure it's Haller's secretary, Gladys Primm. Then a man's voice chimes in, reverberating in the stairwell and somewhat distorted, but I'd know it anywhere. Keeping out of sight, I look up and catch a glimpse of my old friend, Detective Lieutenant Pete Rodriguez working homicide out of Van Nuys. I catch every other word and not much more before they leave the stair well for the 14th floor, accompanied by two armed uniforms. Then all is quiet. Below there is no activity that I'm aware of.

Quickly I descend to the 5th floor landing, open the door to the fifth floor corridor and duck inside. At the moment the corridor is deserted but my luck doesn't hold for long. As I pass an open office door I hear a voice boom out: "Can I help you?" I stop, then turn as a burly six-footer emerges from that office.

"Can I help you with something?" the man asks, looking me up and down as if I were a hobo with his hand out.

"Looking for Oliver Kemp," I say throwing him my most disarming smile.

"What for?"

"Business."

"What kind of business?" the man persists.

In this world there are some of us who were born to be hall monitors and some who were not. This guy clearly belongs to the first group and now I am waiting for him to ask for my pass.

"Lew asked me to come down here and check Rider B, subsection 3 on Peter Falk's contract for the *Columbo* movie."

"Lew?" the guy asks me warily.

"Lew Wasserman," I say, "and why are you busting my chops? By the way, what's your name?"

Color is draining from this blusterer's face.

"We've been told to look out for strange faces—"

"Does my face look strange to you?"

"No, but—"

"Then where can I find Oliver Kemp and don't waste any more of my time."

He points.

"End of the hall, office on the right," he gulps.

I toss him a dirty look, don't bother to thank him, and continue on my way down the corridor. I learned this sort of gamesmanship from a young actor, more often than not out of work, who would walk onto a studio lot in shirt sleeves carrying an official looking clipboard hoping to run into a producer or director with a new project to cast. Silly? Maybe but in a business which is riddled with chutzpah, not an unworthy approach. The young man's not yet a star but he works a lot more than he used to.

There's a name plate in a slot next to the door at the end of the hall. Oliver T. Kemp. I don't bother to knock but just walk right in. A white-haired old lady is sitting at a huge desk in the middle of the room, bent over, holding a magnifying glass and perusing the contents of a Daily Variety, most likely today's. She looks up with a smile. The brass plaque on her desk identifies her as Alma Kitchener.

"Hello. May I help you?" A lace collar is attached to her simple navy blue dress and a I catch a whiff of lavender.

"I'm looking for Oliver Kemp."

"May I ask what about?"

I give her the same line of dishwater I handed the guy in the corridor

She points to a closed door behind her. "Don't bother to knock. I'm sure he's awake by now." She reconsiders. "No, maybe I had better go with you, just in case," she says

We start for the door and as we do I look about me. The room is floor to ceiling with shelves and on the shelves, stacks and stacks of trades and movie magazines, TV Guides, and newspaper sections dedicated to the arts. Charlie wasn't kidding when he said the guy was a little squirrelly. We reach the doorway. Alma goes in first and I linger in the open door frame, looking around at the contents of this second room which are very similar to the first. Fan magazines, trade papers, old newspapers and family magazines with one exception. One set of shelves holds what appears to be the *Encyclopedia Brittanica A to Z* as well as a complete set of law books for the State of California.

An old man who looks a lot like Edmund Gwenn, who played Santa Claus in 'Miracle on 34th Street', is lying on a sofa, snoring quietly. Alma shakes him gently and his eyes open and groggily he sits up. She whispers in his ear and suddenly his back stiffens and he looks at me in disgust as if I had just written something nasty on a men's room wall.

"Liar!" he shouts as he struggles to his feet and starts toward me. "Liar!" he shouts again waving a fist in my direction. "There is no Rider B on the Falk service contract and certainly no subsection 3. Who are you, sir. and how dare you come into my office flying false colors?"

I hand him my card, then calmly and apologetically explain my reason for subterfuge, citing the inquisitive bully in the corridor.

"In reality I have come on behalf of Mr. Wasserman to do some research on Gregory Lunsford, specifically a profile in an edition of Weekly Variety that appeared about two months ago." Another lie but one less likely to trip me up.

"Mae Marsh," Oliver says sadly.

"What?"

"A brilliant actress, a dear heart, a friend I was fortunate to know if only slightly. Miss Marsh left us on February 13th. Her final tribute appeared in the subsequent issue of weekly Variety along with that ridiculous puff piece on Mr. Lunsford."

"You're speaking of her obituary," I say.

He glares at me.

"Young man, the *L.A. Times* prints obituaries, weekly Variety prints tributes."

"Yes, of course. My mistake," I say.

"Yesterday, they featured a heartwarming farewell to Fay Bainter. I actually wept."

"Yes, I'm sure. Now I wonder if—"

"Naturally you have no idea who I am talking about."

"State Fair, Journey for Margaret, The Human Comedy, The Virginian, Mother Carey's Chickens, to name but a few, and of course, Jezebel, 1938, for which she won the Academy Award for playing Aunt Belle Massey."

Now, as if Mae Marsh wasn't enough, he is beginning to tear up over Fay Bainter.

"My apologies, sir," Oliver says. "I misjudged you badly."

"Not at all," I say.

"I'm sure you think me quite silly but these were the ladies I grew up with and one of the reasons I am a self-appointed keeper of the flame. Believe it or not all this collected research material has proved invaluable in many cases in the drawing up of contracts or resolution of disputes."

"Yes, I'm sure—"

"What widow of what major star received nothing in the way of inheritance when I was able to show with my files that said widow was previously married and that said marriage was never terminated making said second marriage a non-marriage and the issue of such non-marriage, two boys and a girl and, well, sir, I invite you to choose your own description of their status. And no, I am not going to tell you who it is."

"I get it, Oliver, and it's obvious you are here doing the Lord's work but right now I have got to read the profile on Greg Lunsford so if you could be so good as to produce that issue of Variety—"

"No problem," Oliver says rising to his feet. He crosses to a nearby shelf, riffles through the pile and carefully extracts a copy from February.

"Be very careful, Mr. Bernardi. The aging process has begun," he says handing me the copy. "You may use that desk over there but obviously I cannot permit you to take the periodical from the room."

"Understandable. I'll let you know when I'm finished."

I go to the desk, flip on the green-shaded lamp and open to the Lunsford article. Oliver exits, sufficiently napped and ready to once again deal with the peccadilloes of America's beloved idols.

Knowing the little I already know about Lunsford, it's a lousy piece of work even for a puff piece and almost certainly didn't involve much if any research. I suspect a lot of it was dictated to Klinger by Lunsford and Klinger wrote what he was told without question. Lunsford was born and raised in rural Georgia. His parents were itinerant farm workers and during his early years his mother taught him to read and write. Without roots, the family left no mark on the state and archives show no mention of a family named Lunsford. He left home when he was 15 and bummed around doing odd jobs and sleeping in barns. There is a passing reference to a stay in Mobile where he worked the fishing boats using his birth name which, if Klinger had learned it, he never specified or was perhaps told not to reveal it. He was known to his friends as Garry or Irish because of his reddish-blonde hair. No mention is made of Dublin, Georgia, being his home for the first fifteen years of his life. Another glaring omission was Garry's friendship with Nathan Halperin. His closest buddies were boat mates and bar flies that hung around the waterfront saloons but no names were cited. He was also enrolled in a theater workshop at a local community college under the name Gregory Lunsford, the first time he had used it. He started writing little dramatic scripts for the group and when he moved on, a letter of recommendation from the theater producer got him in the door at the radio station in Tulsa. Greg Lunsford was on his way.

The narrative becomes increasingly sycophantic. Flowery adjectives abound. His work was always superior, his ideas brilliant. He was beloved and respected by all who came in contact with him. The circuitous route by which he arrived at Universal is covered in broad, laudatory strokes. This is not so much a chronicle as it is a love letter and I wonder why Variety's editors considered it fit to be published. Then I leaf through the rest of the paper and find three full page ads lauding praise on Lunsford's three successful Universal shows. Question asked and answered as judges are wont to say.

I set the paper aside and stand up, stretching. I know for sure there is a link between Haller and Lunsford that goes back a long way though what it is exactly I don't know. Since Klinger glossed over it, it has to be something really damning. Once I get Klinger to tell me about it, even if it costs dearly I will have Lunsford's motive for doing away with Haller. Blackmail is a dirty business that seldom leads to a pastoral retirement overlooking an ocean view.

I return the paper to its stack and exit for the outer room, thanking Oliver for his help which I will certainly mention to Mr. Wasserman. Oliver and Alma are practically glowing when I leave his office for the corridor.

I hurry to the door for the stairs and pull it open, immediately aware that the search party from the lobby has reached the floor below. I hear snatches of conversation. Someone, a man with a booming voice, says this whole thing's a complete waste of time. A woman tells him to shut up. The eyewitnesses are in the grip of acrimony. I look up. Gladys Primm is on her way down accompanied by Pete Rodriguez. I am literally in the jaws of a nutcracker. I fear for my nuts.

I step out into the corridor. All clear. I go in search of refuge— a rest room, a broom closet— anything that will provide me some sort of cover. I pass an open door. Three woman are grouped around a television set. The anchor is announcing that the people in the Tower are being slowly released one at a time from a lobby exit. Tempers are no longer flaring. Civility reigns. Just then I hear voices in the corridor far behind me. The group from below has just arrived. The man with the booming voice is still griping and he's heading my way. I'm standing next to a Ladies Room. Abandoning caution I grab the doorknob and bolt inside. Five stalls, five sinks and otherwise empty.

I dash to the far stall, go in and close the door, then stand on the seat and scrunch down. From the outside this will look like an empty stall. If someone opens the stall door, I am dead meat and there will be an asterisk next to my name shouting 'pervert'. I stoop frozen in place listening to muffled voices from the corridor. The man for sure though I can't really hear what is being said. I strain. No good. Then suddenly the voices are loud and clear. Someone has opened the corridor door.

"Hello? Anybody here? Yoo hoo." A woman's voice. A pause, then: "No one there." And then the voices are muffled again as the door swings shut. The garbled babble continues, then grows fainter as the search party ambles down the corridor checking out each room. My knees are locked up, my neck is stiff, my feet have grown numb. I am about to step cautiously off the toilet seat when the corridor noise leaps to life. Someone has just opened the door and entered. Again I freeze stock still. I hear high heels on the marble floor, then quiet. I am holding my breath.

Suddenly the stall door is flung wide open and I find myself face to face with a beautiful blonde. Her eyes open wide, startled, Her mouth opens as well. I wait for the scream. I hear only a gasp and then: "Joe?"

"Holly?" I say in disbelief.

"What are you doing?" she asks.

"Hiding."

"They say there's a mad dog killer on the loose," Holly says.

"That would be me," I say.

"No!" she says in disbelief

"Yes," I reply. "But they have it wrong."

"Of course they do," she responds.

"I need help."

"Okay."

"I have to get out of this building. Can you help me?"

"Sure," she smiles.

Hourglass Holly Hoopes is one of the sweetest girls I know, all peaches and cream and cuddly and boasting an IQ very close to her body temperature. She has been looking for Mister Right for over a decade now but she keeps getting saddled with a batch of Mr. Wrongs. I should know. Many years ago I was one of them for about a month before she traded me in for a very successful television idol whose IQ was even lower than hers. I think some of the words I used were too big for her.

Gently she helps me down from the commode and leads me to the door. She opens it, looks both ways, and then tugging at me, we duck into the corridor, hurry two doors down and enter a private office belonging to Preston Gould, Vice President of Foreign Sales and Syndication.

"Is this safe?" I ask apprehensively as she flips on the lights.

"Don't worry, Pressie is out playing golf with the boys. Follow me."

She leads me across the outer office and we go into what turns out to be Pressie's private office featuring a huge mahogany desk and an even huger three section sofa. She brings me to a closet which contains a couple of spare suits, two sports jackets, shirts, ties, socks and underwear and several golf caps.

"Sometimes Pressie stays overnight with a business associate and it's more convenient to have a change of clothes here than to drive all the way to Bel Air to shower and change."

I nod, seeing the wisdom of such an arrangement.

"Would you be that business associate, Holly?"

"Of course," she says, taking down a camel's hair sport jacket for me to try on. "How are things with you, Joe? Did you ever catch up with that babe you were chasing all over the country?"

"Caught her, hogtied her, brought her home and married her."

Holly grins.

"Terrific, Joe. I love happy endings."

"How's it with you, Holly? Any luck on your end?"

"Not much. It pretty much comes down to Pressie."

"Married?"

"What else? 24 years."

"Kids?"

"Four. Two in college."

"Is he getting ready to divorce his wife?"

"Naw, I told him to save his breath. I've heard that old story a few thousand times from a few thousand guys. "

"You're better than that, Holly," I say.

"No, I'm not. Lotta good stuff in here. We can fix you up real well, Joe." She pulls a cap down from the shelf and hands it to me. L.A. Lakers. Dark blue. I try it on. Decent fit.

Just then we hear voices coming from the anteroom just as the corridor door was opening.

"Anybody in there?"

"Don' t see anyone."

"Lights on. Must mean something," says a guy with a gravelly voice.

"Hello? Anybody home?"

"Maybe in the other room."

Holly grabs my arm and hauls me across the room, whispering as she does,"Take your shirt off! Take off your damned shirt!" She pushes me onto the large sofa and starts to rip off her blouse. "Now. Take it off!" I tug at my tie and pull it off, then go to work on my shirt as Holly unsnaps her bra and flings it away.

"I'll check the other room."

She dives onto the sofa and takes me in her arms and instinctively I reciprocate just as the door opens.

"Hey!" the man says from the open doorway.

Holly whips her head around, looks at him and screams loud enough to awaken Dracula from his coffin.

"Jesus, lady!" he says. The gravely voiced guy.

"Get out! You hear me, you son of a bitch! Get out!" Then, to me more quietly but loud enough to be heard: "Keep your head down, Mr. Gould. Don't let the bastard see your face!" She turns her attention back to the gravely voiced guy who has now been joined by a woman and a studio security officer.

"I'm sorry, Miss—"

"Sorry? Don't give me that crap!" She stands up, folding her arms across her naked bosom. "Where's the son of a bitch with the camera? Show your face, you bastard!"

"Ma'am, you don't understand—"

"When is that bitch going to get the message? No divorce. No how. Never. And you people can take your camera and shove it ! Go! Now get out!"

I'm peeking through my fingers as the interlopers start to back off. Holly turns her venom on the security guy.

"And you," she says, "don't you like your job? Wait til Dr. Stein hears about this. You'll be eating your meals at a soup kitchen in Boyle Heights!"

"We're going!" the security guy says. "Didn't mean to invade your privacy. Very sorry about all this, Mr. Gould!" he shouts in my direction. Staying concealed I give him an acknowledging wave and then the three of them are gone. I hear the outer door close and only then do I pop my head up. Holly and I stay perfectly still for what seems an eon and finally she turns to me.

"You want to finish what we started?" she asks with a smile.

"Can't," I reply.

"Wife?"

"You bet."

"Guess Pressie wouldn't be too happy about it either," she sighs as she looks around for her bra.

"That was pretty quick thinking, Holly," I say.

She shrugs.

"A lotta years, Joe. I've had enough practice," she says, somewhat sadly.

CHAPTER ELEVEN

I take a hard look at myself in Preston Gould's bathroom mirror and if I do say so myself, I look pretty damned good: Lakers cap, sunglasses, camel hair sport jacket over my dark suit pants. I could be Cary Grant trying to avoid his adoring public. I know for sure I don't look much like Joe Bernardi. I have a better than even chance of getting out of this building without being grabbed.

Holly takes my arm.

"Come on, gorgeous, let's get you out of here," she says.

"Me, not you," I say, shrugging her off. "You've done enough already."

"I certainly have," she says, "but I'm having such a good time, I don't want it to end. Believe me, Pressie isn't this much fun."

"Cops are involved. They think I killed someone. Just being seen with me could mess up your life."

"Hey, Joe," she says. "Pay close attention. It's already messed up. I'm going with you at least until you're out the door and free and clear. Otherwise I will follow behind you, pointing, and yelling 'That's him! That's him!'"

"You wouldn't."

"Try me."

"All right, all right," I say, shaking my head in surrender. "We do it your way. Let's go."

She breaks out laughing.

"You're such a pussy, Always were."

She grabs my arm again and we head for the stairwell.

People are coming down the stairs in groups of twos and threes, now that the word is out that departure through the lobby is possible. I get jostled and look to my right. Levinson and Link are fleeing the premises with unseemly haste and I fix Link with a hard stare behind my sepia lenses.

"Watch it, buddy!" I say sharply.

He looks right at me, mutters an apology and moves on. I was with the guy less than an hour ago and he doesn't recognize me. My hopes buoy. I feel like Frank Morris, the only con ever to escape from Alcatraz prison.

It takes just over six minutes to descend from the fifth floor to the lobby which is overflowing with ill-tempered employees and visitors anxious to escape this purgatory. Crowd control is being handled by studio officers and Jake McElrath, the chief of security, is positioned a few feet from the one exit door, watching carefully as the so-called 'eyewitnesses' do their thing. Bill Link I just met. McElrath I have known casually for a couple of years. He may not be so easy to fool.

From behind my sunglasses my eyes flit left and right. I spot at least a dozen people I know on a first name business but so far none have recognized me. Holly and I shuffle forward as lines merge. A cute receptionist type looks over at her with a smile.

"Hey, Holly, who's the hunk?"

"None of your damned business, Charlotte. I found him at the tennis club and he's all mine. Ain't you, honey?" she says to me.

"If you say so, darlin', " I respond with a trace of Alabama.

A heavy-set woman at the head of the line starts jawing at one of McElrath's security guys. The line stops. Irritated voices start to excoriate the woman who says something unrepeatable, displays her middle finger to a vociferous Sparklett's water delivery guy and then imperiously waddles out the door. The milk of human kindness seems sorrowfully in short supply this lovely Spring day.

At last we reach the head of the line. The open doorway is just a few feet away as are four eyewitnesses, two men and two woman and a security guy holding a copy of the infamous photograph which makes me look like a cross between Rosalind Russell and Merle Oberon. One eyewitness jabs another pointing excitedly to a man about fifteen back in the line. The other shakes his head. The one insists. Glares are exchanged. While they are arguing Holly and I glide past unmolested and step out into the fresh air. We elbow our way through the crowd of gawkers and head for the commissary which is close by. Two TV stations are on the job and on-air reporters are trying to grab hold of anyone who will talk to them. The cops and the security guys are trying to maintain some semblance of order but one of the TV guys reaches out for me. I shrug him off.

Holly and I have just reached the outer limits of the crowd. Next stop, my car which is parked near Stage 15. I am just removing my sunglasses when I hear him shouting.

"That's him! That's the mutha tried to beat up on that old man."

I look to my left. The black actor, Denny Crowe, is pointing at me. "That's him. I'd know him anywhere. Threatened to kill the old buzzard. Yeah, that's right. I heard him say it."

Two nearby cops have heard him and now they're looking at me. Instinctively I back away. Bad move. Their eyes light up. They step toward me. Leaving Holly behind I dash away, make my way up the street, trying to mix in with the traffic and the busses and the extras. I duck down a narrow alley and keep running, sticking to the shadows which are starting to envelope the narrow back alleys between stages. I find myself gasping for air and holding my side. Still I plow forth, confident but not positive that I have shaken my pursuers. Finally I stop, gulping in air, pressing back into the shadows of sound stage 28 where years ago Universal filmed the Lon Chaney version of 'The Phantom of the Opera' and then a remake during the war starring Nelson Eddy sans Jeanette MacDonald. I hear shouted voices far off but moving closer.

I need to gather my strength. The way I'm breathing further running is out of the question. I am standing by a doorway to the sound stage which is unquestionably locked but when I try the knob, it gives and the door swings open. Quickly I duck inside, shutting the door behind me.

It is dim inside the cavernous sound stage as sunlight tries to force its way in through a few dirt encrusted windows. There is dust everywhere and I am unable to stifle a sneeze. The aging process has brought me few blessings but one thing it has given me is a pronounced allergy to dust and pollen. I sneeze again. This is not good. I am at the back of the stage looking out toward the orchestra and the balcony and high above, the infamous chandelier which halfway through the performance comes crashing down onto the audience. As my eyes grow accustomed to the darkness, I look around for a decent place to hide. My pursuers may not come in but if I could find an open door, so can they.

Now I hear voices coming near. Very near. They are right outside. I consider hiding in one of the theater boxes that look down on the stage but I don't know where the stairs are and there is too much loose debris around for me to fumble in the darkness, inviting a noisy fall and perhaps a broken bone or two. To the side, stacked against the padded wall, are dozens of flats. A flat is a piece of scenery, invariably a section of a 'wall'. a light wooden frame over which canvas has been pulled taut. With the proper lighting a set made up of flats can appear to be as substantial as the halls of Congress.

A doorknob rattles. A voice shouts out 'Locked! Try around back!' I dart over to the flats which are 12 feet high. I tug at the outer one and I am able to move it enough to be able to slide in behind it. Sandwiched between the two flats I am not visible. The trick will be to not move and more importantly, not sneeze.

I stand stock still and a few moments later I hear the rear door open and now the voices are loud and clear.

"You sure he ducked in here?"

"Hell, no, but it won't hurt to look. The guy's not going anywhere."

"Says you. We don't even know who he is."

"Yeah, well, all I know is, if he slips away, Jake's gonna have our asses."

Good news. These are two of Jake McElrath's security force and probably less formidable than two LAPD uniforms. Suddenly my nose begins to twitch. I bring my hand to my nose and squeeze tight, stifling the urge.

"Nobody here, Bo."

"Not so sure about that."

"And if he is, we're not going to find him. Not in this darkness with all this crap laying around."

"Yeah, I guess you're right. Let's go."

I hear them moving around and then the rear door opens, light pours in and then the door closes and once more it is eerily quiet inside the building. I stay very still for an eternity which was probably more like five minutes. I stifled every sneeze but one but it attracted no interest. I come out from behind the flat and check my watch. Quarter past five. If I had half a brain I'd stay hidden until darkness settles in but that's not an option. I'm supposed to meet the writer, Brett Klinger, at Chasen's restaurant at six o'clock and this is a date I have to keep. I slip out of the sports jacket, cap and sunglasses and pile them on a table. Later I'll call Holly and tell her where she can find them. I exit the sound stage the way I came in and go in search of officialdom. What is needed now is a brazen approach, running and skulking will get me nowhere except a private room at the Van Nuys lockup facility.

As I head back toward the commissary I spot Jake McElrath talking to one of the LAPD uniforms. No time like the present, I think, and I jog toward him.

"Jake!" I shout. He turns toward me as I reach him breathless. "Help!" I say with a grin.

"What happened, Joe, you lose your suit jacket?" he asks with an amused smile.

"Funny, Jake, but I know exactly where my jacket is. In the boot of my car. Trouble is I was locked up in the Bastille so long I forgot where I parked it. And I've got a dinner date at six o'clock."

"Now that's a problem," Jake says, then looks past me. "Hey, Bo!"

I turn. Jake is shouting at one of the two security guys who chased me into stage 28.

"You seen Mr. Bernardi's car parked anywhere? The cream colored Bentley with the right hand drive?"

"I think I seen it over by 15 but I wouldn't swear to it."

Jake looks at me with a smile.

"Okay?"

"Thanks," I say and start off in the direction of stage 15.

"Joe!" Jake says sharply. I look back at him. "Don't you want to know?"

"Know what?"

"The guy. Did we catch him?"

"Oh. No, uh, I heard you missed him."

"Where'd you hear that?"

"I don't know. I think two guys walking by me when I'm looking for my car. Why? Were they wrong? Did you grab him?"

Jake shakes his head.

"No, he got by us. Maybe we should have had that actor of yours helping us. Falk. I hear he makes a pretty good cop."

"You hear right, Jake. See ya."

I give him a little wave and hurry off to retrieve my car.

I find it right where I left it alongside stage 15. I slip behind the wheel, fire her up and pull away from the building. I make one turn and then a beeline for the main gate. It is relatively quiet, the crowds have dispersed and Scotty is waving everybody through, anxious I'm sure to be done with the high drama of the past few hours. I check my watch again. Twenty to six. I have to go over the hill into Hollywood then scoot over to Beverly Boulevard in West Hollywood. I'll never make it but maybe Klinger's taken me up on that free meal I offered him.

I get lucky. I drive up at ten after, turn my car over to the valet and hurry inside. Chasen's is a legendary hangout for the powerful and famous and those who'd like to be but, because of the hour, they have yet to arrive and hang out. Klinger is sitting in a rear booth, tossing down a highball. I start toward him but Leonardo, the maitre'd stops me.

"Uh, Mr. Bernardi, I'm sorry, but-- uh—your jacket, sir."

I immediately realize I am breaking a house rule. Jacket and tie required. I've got the tie. I don't got the jacket.

"Darn. Sorry, Leo, I spilled coffee on it at lunch and dropped it off at a dry cleaner."

"Of course, sir. I'm sure I have something for you. An 18 long I would say. Just one moment." He disappears into the coat room and emerges a few moments later with a gaudy yellow-brown herringbone. "I think this should do it, Mr. Bernardi." He holds it up for me to slip into.

"Couldn't you have found me something a little uglier, Leo?"

"I tried, sir, but this is the best I could do," he says dryly. "The good news is, at this ungodly hour, there is no one here to see you in it."

And as I said, he's right. At a few minutes past six there's no one around except for a few out of town tourists trying to experience the high life and four or five wannabe actors or starlets or whatever waiting for the appearance of somebody --anybody--who could do something for their careers. Me, I'm here to have dinner with a third-rate hack writer named Brett Klinger.

"Sorry I'm late," I say, slipping into the booth opposite him. I thank Leonardo who drifts away.

"It's okay," Klinger says. "Six o'clock came and I ordered. Figured you wouldn't mind."

"Delighted," I say.

A waiter slides noiselessly up to the table, laying a menu in front of me.

"Good evening, sir. My name is Frederick and it will be my pleasure to serve you this evening," he says.

"Lovely," I say. "And my name is Joseph, Freddie, and it will be my pleasure to be served."

Frederick's face stiffens subtly, obviously surprised that we are already on a first name basis.

"May I bring you something to drink, sir?" he asks.

"Certainly. A cold Coors in a long neck, hold the glass."

"Very good, sir," he says and glides away.

Somebody ought to tell Dave Chasen about this guy. Before he delved into the restaurant business, Dave was a professional comedian, a very funny guy. Frederick is not. If not stopped Freddie's going to give the place a bad name.

"So—" I say.

"So," Klinger replies, "you said something about a C-note, Mr. Bernardi?"

"So I did," I say, reaching into my wallet and plucking out a hundred dollar bill which I slide across the table. Klinger palms it and slides it into his shirt pocket. "My lobster will be arriving momentarily. Thanks for that as well."

"My pleasure."

"Now about my article," Klinger says. "What did you think?"

"Not much. You took dictation and little else."

"Accurate, Mr. Bernardi, but I was not expecting critical kudos. I am a middle man in a morass of mediocrity. I write third rate material about third rate people for a decent enough publication, saving the excrement for a third rate scandal rag which pays handsomely, and even more handsomely the smellier the excrement. I don't delude myself that what I do is anything more."

"Not mentioning his college, that was a big omission."

"He wouldn't tell me. Said it was a very small Lutheran college in Wyoming, hardly prestigious. He said he would have been embarrassed by it."

"But not too embarrassed to wear a Phi Beta Kappa key," I say. "I wonder where he got it. The Harvard gift shop?"

"He said he was valedictorian of a class of 54 with a 4.6 grade average. He said it wasn't hard. Half the rubes were dumb and the other half didn't care."

"One thing I'm troubled by," I say. "Why do you suppose Variety published your piece?" I ask.

"No idea unless Haller has photos of the editor and his six year old granddaughter playing Doctor and Nurse."

I shake my head.

"No, I don't think even Nate Haller would—"

"Wise up, Bernardi!" Klinger says sharply. "You obviously don't know the first thing about Nate Haller. Vermin want nothing to do with him."

Frederick returns with my cold, uncapped bottle of Coors which he sets down before me.

"Would you care to order, sir?" he asks.

"I'll tell you, Freddie, I'm not all that hungry just now. Keep an eye on the table and if I change my mind, I'll give you the high sign."

"Very good, sir."

"Joe. It's Joe, Freddie. Call me Joe."

"Yes, sir. Of course, sir--sir Joe." He spins away and hotfoots it toward the kitchen ignoring an attractive woman and her husband who have been trying to get his attention for the past twenty minutes.

"Okay, Brett. Let's get to core of this apple. You learned something damning about Greg Lunsford withheld it from Variety and sold it for a handsome fee to Nate Keller who in turn squeezed a donation to his slush fund from Lunsford for keeping his mouth shut."

"Not precisely correct, Mr. Bernardi. For one of the few times in my life I couldn't do business with Haller."

An obvious lie but why.

"But you found out something about Lunsford," I say.

"I did and it was pretty incendiary stuff but Haller claimed he already knew about it."

"Knew about what?"

"Years ago in Mobile, Lunsford was allegedly involved with some other guys in a bar brawl in which a man was killed. Lunsford was questioned but before he could be arrested, he skipped town. Haller said that that rumor was floated a decade ago by a rival producer and nothing came of it. In any event Haller made it clear he wasn't going to pay good money for yesterday's news." He smiles. "You, on the other hand, Mr. Bernardi—"

"I'm not interested, either, Mr. Klinger. Since I actually bothered to dig into it, I probably know more about that bar fight than you do and about the kid nicknamed Irish because he was born in Dublin, Georgia, christened Garry Leden before he changed it. No, Lunsford skipped all that in his dictation to you and for good reason. He had no intention of being dragged back to Alabama to answer for a twenty year old murder."

"More than a rumor, then?" Klinger says.

"Yes."

Klinger hesitates and a sly smile crosses his lips.

"I apologize, Mr. Bernardi. I badly underestimated you. Here are the facts as I was able to dig them up. The date was February 23, 1941, a dive called the Bucket of Grog. The victim was named John Kingsley, Detective First Grade Little Rock Police Department. Others involved Garry Leden, Nathan Halperin, a Cuban national named Santiago, since disappeared, and a ship's cook named Obermann who died in 1944 in a U-Boat attack in the North Atlantic."

I nod.

"And apparently I short-changed you, Brett."

"I think I knew right away that Halperin and Haller were one and the same person, and then when he refused to buy the information, that confirmed it."

"Strange, though," I say, puzzled. "Haller couldn't use that information against Lunsford without implicating himself."

"Lunsford was wealthy and successful with years of prosperity ahead of him. I think Haller gambled that Lunsford wouldn't take the chance and he was right. I think Lunsford paid once and now was being pressured to pay again. For Lunsford that was one time too many."

Frederick approaches the table, carrying Klinger's dinner as if it were the crown jewels of England, and sets it down. The lobster, having changed color from sea green to a lustrous red, has seen better days. Klinger's eyes brighten and he throws me a smile. I can only think of the words 'market price'.

I drain my beer and then slip out of the booth.

"It's been informative, Brett. Thanks. And bon appetit."

I turn and walk out of the restaurant.

CHAPTER TWELVE

It's been a miserable day and all I want to do is go home and hug and kiss my gorgeous wife and my precocious and bubbly 14 year old daughter. It isn't all that far from Chasen's to home but the traffic is crappy and the stop-and-go is grating on my nerves and wearing on my patience. It's nearly seven o'clock when I am able to turn onto Franklin Avenue. Dinner time has probably come and gone but if not, I am determined to take everyone out for a relaxing supper at Biff's All-American Diner, a treat for everyone. I may even let Bridget tag along.

And then I see it and my gut tightens into a knot. This lousy day is far from over. A cruiser marked Universal Studios Security is parked in front of our house and a dozen reasons for it to be there spring to mind, none of them good. I keep rolling past and then cut down to Hollywood and Vine where I pull up in front of Ziggy's drug store. The only thing I need from Ziggy this evening is his phone booth. Three rings and then Bunny picks up.

"Hello," she says.

"I just drove by the house. I see we have company." I say.

She takes a moment to put it together, then says: "He's not here but I'm expecting him. I think he was spending the day at Universal. Can I give him a message?"

"Who's with you? McElrath?"

"I believe so."

"Alone?"

"Yes."

I think for a moment.

"Put him on the phone."

"What's going on?"

"Things are complicated but I'm okay."

"Nate Haller's dead," she says.

"I know."

"Is that why McElrath is here?"

"Probably."

"Oh, my God, Joe—"

"I'll be okay, Bunny. Promise. Put him on the phone."

"Are you sure?"

"Can't run, can't hide. Let me speak to him."

A long silence and then McElrath comes on the line.

"Joe?"

"If I'd known you were going to stop by, I'd have been there to welcome you."

"Last minute thing. We need to talk."

"What about?"

"Your suit jacket for one thing. We found it in Preston Gould's office, not in the boot of your car."

"Who's we?"

"Me and Bo Ransome."

"Not Rodriguez?"

"He'd already gone back to his headquarters. I wasn't about to bother him about something that can easily be explained away."

"Of course it can and by the way, Holly Hoopes has nothing to do with this."

"Who said she did? You stumbled into an office where the exec liked to keep extra wardrobe in the closet. Come home, Joe, We need to talk."

"No. I don't want my family involved. I'll meet you."

"Where?"

"The Observatory. Eight o'clock. Come alone."

"I can do that," McElrath says. "Joe, don't stiff me. I'm on your side in this."

"Good to hear."

"Eight o'clock," he says, "and don't be late." He hangs up.

The Griffith Observatory is an iconic L.A. landmark located on the east face of Mount Hollywood in Griffith Park. It was made famous in the James Dean film 'Rebel Without a Cause' and has been used as a location in countless films since then. At this time of the evening it will be crawling with people. The Planetarium Theater runs programs every evening until ten p.m. If Jake McElrath is planning something stupid, this will definitely be the wrong time and place to try it.

The parking lot at the observatory is small and at this time in the evening it will be full so I do what everyone else does. I park at the side of the long driveway leading to the main building. I bypass two empty spots at the bottom of the hill, then find another halfway up. I decide not to press my luck and pull in and park. It's quarter to eight, plenty of time to get to the entrance and linger unobserved to see if McElfrath arrives alone. As I trudge up the driveway a late model Pontiac Le Mans shoots by me headed for the parking lot. No doubt a tourist. He'll be back. And sure enough, a minute later, here he comes. But then he does a strange thing. He stops about twenty yards in front of me, hops out of his car, and hurries toward me. When he gets close, I notice the gun in his hand. When he gets really close, I recognize his face. It belongs to Bart Kane, Nate Haller's bodyguard.

"I'd prefer not to shoot you, Joe, so please, no fuss, no heroics.

Just come with me."

"What's the problem, Bart?" I ask.

"At the moment, you are. Walk to my car. Now."

At this hour the light is fading but I can see his face clearly and his eyes reveal a deep rooted desperation. This is a man with nothing to lose. I don't hesitate. I walk past him to his double-parked car and start toward the passenger side.

"Other side, Joe," Kane says. "You're driving."

I open the driver side door and slip behind the wheel. Kane gets in the passenger side and hands me the keys. "Drive," he says. He doesn't have to tell me twice.

"Where are we going?" I ask.

"The office."

"Yours or mine?"

He gives me a hard look.

"You always were a wise guy, Joe."

"Just can't help it," I reply, and head the car for the 'Hollywood Exposed' offices on Vermont Avenue. Twice I try to start a conversation and twice Kane remains mute, staring quietly ahead through the window. I try for a third time to find out what Kane is up to. This time Kane glares at me.

"If I'd wanted to spend my life in conversation, Joe, I would have gotten married. Shut up and drive."

A few minutes later I turn onto Vermont Avenue. The office building looms up on the left.

"Go past the building, left at the corner, park on the side street."

I do as I'm told and then hand Kane the keys. We exit the car and start back to the building, Kane slightly behind me holding the gun which is barely visible. At the front entrance, Kane uses a key to open the door into a lobby which is lit with low level lighting. He prods me inside and we go to the elevator well, then take it to the third floor. Still nothing from Kane aside from an occasional grunt. He uses another key to let us into the office. He flips on the lights and gestures toward a nearby chair. I step toward it and sit just as the connecting door opens and Claudia Hicks barges into the room holding a small caliber pistol."

"Whoa!!" Kane says, startled.

"What are you doing here, Bart?" she demands to know.

"The same thing you are, Toots."

"And why'd you bring him into this?" she asks, nodding toward me.

"I think he knows something."

"I seriously doubt that. Joe's one of the good guys, Bart. Trust me."

"Haller's dead. Bernardi either killed him or was one of the last people to see him alive. I've been following him ever since he left Chasen's. He goes home but drives by when he sees the cops are there, then heads for a drug store to make a phone call, all of this being very suspicious, and then he heads for the observatory, equally suspicious."

"Joe didn't kill anybody and put away that gun," she says.

Reluctantly he does so.

"Only because you say so, babe. You didn't find anything, did you?" Kane says.

"You know I didn't," Claudia says.

"Excuse me," I say, cautiously raising my hand. "Would one of you tell me what's going on around here?"

"We're looking for hidden treasure, Joe," Kane says.

"Haller's secret files. The ones he shared with no one," Claudia says.

"The file with the goods on Greg Lunsford," I venture.

"Among others," Claudia says.

"Among others including the two of you?" I ask.

They look at each other but say nothing.

"Okay, I get the picture," I say, nodding. "Your files, my wife's file, we're all on the same page."

"I saw you go into the bank, Joe," Kane says. "Maybe you did him, maybe you didn't. I know if I had a wife like yours I'd give it a lot of thought. In any case he might have said something to you before he died, Claudia and I both need to burn some papers."

I look from one to the other. These two are no threat. They are not dangerous. If anything they are scared to death. Haller, as sharp as he was, would have been extra cautious to protect himself, perhaps by giving them to an attorney or a close friend with the admonition, 'In the event of my death for whatever reason' and so forth.

"Let's get a couple of things straight. One, I don't have the files. Two, I did not push your boss off the roof. Three, I have a pretty good idea who did but unless I can prove it, I'm the target of the day."

"Who?"

"Gregory Lunsford."

"He was there," Claudia says. "They showed some of the bank lobby tapes on the news."

"Yeah, and I saw him go inside," Kane says.

"All mussed up, suit soiled, as if he'd fallen in the parking lot?" I suggest.

"I didn't see anything like that," Kane says.

"Neither did I," I reply, "which means he got messed up in a struggle on the roof. Had to be that way."

"Maybe Haller revealed something to Lunsford," Kane suggests.

"I don't think so," I say. "Whatever Haller had on Lunsford isn't in the files. It didn't have to be."

"You sound like you know something we don't, Joe," Claudia says.

"I do, Claudia, and Lunsford doesn't need to acquire the files to protect himself. But he might want them for another reason."

"Continue the blackmail," Kane says.

"It's a possibility," I say. "Not that Lunsford needs the money, he doesn't, but information is power and Lunsford is just the type that would acquire it and use it in any way it might benefit him."

"All the more reason we need to find the files and destroy them," Claudia says. "What about his house in Bel Air? Would he keep the files there?"

"He might," Kane says, "but it's a fortress, guarded gates at every entrance, continual patrols, guard dogs, and the house itself may be wired like the Queen's bedroom."

"How are you at fortresses, Bart?" Claudia asks.

"I'm rusty, Toots," he says. "Been a while."

"What's a while?" I ask.

"Six years. Havana, Cuba. The Presidential Palace, recently acquired by Fidel Castro, a few very large villas overlooking the harbor taken over by his thugs. Thanks to my background with the OSS at the end of the war, I was loaned out by the LAPD to that other alphabet organization in Washington. Also, It didn't hurt that my mother is Cuban and I speak it perfectly with the accent."

I look at him with a smile.

"The things you learn about people that you never knew before." I say.

"They wanted me to stay, those alphabet people, but I came back to L.A. first chance I got," Bart says. "Something about that outfit, even a shower twice a day didn't help."

"And Bel Air?" I ask. "Can you handle it?"

"Do I have a choice?" Bart asks.

CHAPTER THIRTEEN

Getting past security at this prestigious gated community proved to be no problem. The guard at the East Gate is a middle aged ex-cop named Chester Riggs and he and Bart have known each other for years. In the days before Bart was loaned out to the alphabet gang in Washington, he and Riggs were partners. Riggs was young and newly married with a kid and needed money so he tried to make a big score with the ponies. It backfired and soon Riggs was in deep in cow dung with both bookmakers and loan sharks. When Bart learned of it, he took care of the problem although not specifying how, making sure that Riggs knew this was a one time thing and never to be repeated. Riggs learned his lesson well and the two of them have been close ever since. After being clued in as to our mission and being reassured that this favor would not come back on him, Riggs opened the gate and allowed us to pass a minute or two past eleven o'clock.

Now we are crawling along Roscoemare Road, searching for the cross street which will lead to Nate Haller's ostentatious three story EnglishTudor nestled on a well landscaped acre and a half. Bart is driving after stopping off at his house to pick up a black satchel which apparently contains the tools of his trade. Hence comes the phrase 'black bag operation' or so I surmise. Bart turns and up ahead on the right, bathed in moonlight, is Haller's home. Bart turns into the driveway.

"Shouldn't we park on the street or something?" I say.

Bart laughs.

"Not in this neighborhood, Joe. Strange cars attract security the way Hershey wrappers attract flies."

He pulls around to the back of the house out of sight, parks, and douses the headlights. He gets out of the car and scans the perimeter. Most of what he sees is Haller's landscaping.

"Quiet enough," he says. "Let's go." He pops the trunk lid and grabs the black satchel, then starts for the rear door. I follow. I've heard plenty about guys like Bart but never seen one in action. Five minutes later I've seen it but I couldn't tell you what he did. I only know he did strange things with wires and batteries and a half dozen electrical appliances and when he was finally done, he turned the door knob and walked inside. No alarm sounded. No glaring lights disturbed the darkness. He beckoned to me and Claudia to follow him in and when we did, he closed the door behind us.

"We're looking for either a wall safe or a secret hiding spot secreted behind one of the walls," Bart says. "I favor the latter and I suspect the bedroom. I may be wrong. I don't think so but if I am we'll start over again on this floor and work our way up."

Claudia and I follow him to the front foyer which is lit with moonbeams coming in through several windows. He's also carrying a huge 4-battery flashlight that lights up the staircase like Coney Island on a Fourth of July weekend. We wend our way to the second floor and poke our noses into several rooms until we come upon a massive master bedroom with an equally massive king sized bed. Six Nathan Hallers could fit into it without crowding.

Bart has Claudia and me checking behind paintings for a wall safe while he slowly circumnavigates the room with a stethoscope in his ears as he taps on the walls. Suddenly he stops. Tap tap. Then tap tap again. A phony Picasso hangs on the wall but there is no wall safe behind it. There should, however, be a hidden cavity. He drops to his knees, starts to feel along the base board moulding. A moment later I hear an audible click and then Bart pushes the wall. A section gives and then slides to the left revealing three deep shelves on which are stacked at least twenty binders and accordion folders. We pull them out just as the phone rings.

We all freeze, looking at one another. Then Bart says,"Pick it up, Joe. It might be Riggs."

I'm right next to the bedside phone. I lift the receiver and hear Riggs' voice.

"Bart? That you?"

"No, Joe Bernardi."

"Whatever you guys just did you tripped a silent alarm. You need to get out of there fast."

"How much time do we have?"

"The alarm comes here and also to the West L.A.Community Police Station. They'll wait for me to call them in case it's just a false alarm. If I don't call within three minutes they dispatch a cruiser. It'll probably take them fifteen minutes but you can't count on it. A cruiser inside the gates could be there immediately so whatever you're doing, drop it and move it."

"Thanks, Riggs," I say, hanging up and repeating the message to my co-conspirators.

"No time to sort," Bart says. "Grab a couple of pillow cases and we'll take it all." I empty two pillow cases from the bed and the three of us cram in Haller's files, then dash for the stairs.

All is quiet as we leave by the back door. The crickets are cricking, the hoot owls hooting but not a peep from any police siren. We toss the pillows into the trunk and Bart starts to gun it out of there, then stops short. There's an opening in the shrubbery ahead of us, somewhat wider than a footpath, that apparently leads to the darkened house to Haller's rear. Bart moves forward, turns and heads down this narrow opening, foliage slapping viciously at both sides of his car as we crawl toward the neighbor's backyard and the end of his driveway. I look back through the rear window. Bart must have a highly developed sixth sense because lights are beginning to play on Haller's driveway. Bart sees it too and cuts his headlights, creeping slowly ahead by the light of the moon. We emerge from the shrubs and Bart cuts over to the neighbor's driveway, then speeds toward the street. It isn't until we are well away from the scene that Bart puts the headlights back on and hustles toward the Sunset Boulevard gate and safety.

It's midnight when we pull into Bart Kane's driveway and tote our pillowcases inside. Bart offers to put on coffee but all Claudia and I want to do is find Haller's filthy blackmail material and destroy it. Bart forgets about the coffee and starts a fire in the fireplace that is the centerpiece of his living room. We sit cross-legged in the middle of the room and, one by one, start pulling the offensive files from the cases. When I have scanned a file long enough to know it doesn't pertain to me or Bunny or Bart or Claudia, I put it aside, fodder for the flames in the fireplace.

We work in silence. Suddenly Claudia stops scanning her folder and hands its to me.

"Yours," she says.

I open it and find Bunny's bleary visage staring up at me. I close it and toss the file onto the burn pile.

"I've got mine," Bart says, adding his folder to the collection.

"Uh oh," Claudia says.

"Yours?" Bart asks.

"Hedda Hopper," she replies.

"No kidding," Bart says. "What's the old babe been up to?"

"Don't know, don't care," Claudia says, adding the Hopper folder to the burn pile.

"And here's yours, Toots," Bart says handing over Claudia's file folder unread. She glances at it, then tosses it atop Hedda.

"Well, that does it," I say.

"Yeah. All present or accounted for," Bart says as he gets to his feet. He takes an armful of material from the burn pile and carries it to the roaring fireplace. "So this is what it feels like to incinerate several million dollars." he says going back for another armload.

A few minutes later it's approaching twelve thirty and we're on the road again, heading back to the Observatory so I can pick up my car. My two companions are relaxed, almost jovial. They have put their nightmares to rest. Whatever the future may hold, it won't include servitude to Nate Haller. Within minutes we turn onto the long driveway that leads up to the Observatory. The place is deserted, everyone's left. There should be only one car parked by the side of the road. There should be but there isn't. My Bentley is gone.

"It was right there," I say waving a finger.

"Are you sure?" Claudia asks.

"It was there," Bart says. "I saw it. You've been towed, Joe."

"Just great," I mutter. There are a few things I can do without in my life. My car isn't one of them.

"I'll give you a ride home," Bart says. "You can call the impound in the morning."

"Beats walking. Thanks, Bart," I say, still pissed.

It's nearly one a.m. when we pull up in front of my house and Bart leaves me off at curbside. I thank him, tell him I'll be in touch and trudge up to the front door where the porch light is lit. I'm pretty sure there's also a light on in the living room. It's been a long day and I am bushed. I crave a good night's sleep. I take one last look back at Bart's departing car as it drives past a dark colored sedan parked at curbside. I vaguely realize I've never seen that car in the neighborhood before but I really don't give it a second thought.

As soon as I walk in the door, I see her. Bunny's in the living room, dressed in a nightgown and bathrobe, curled up in an easy chair asleep. I go to her and kneel down, shaking her gently.

"Hi," I say.

"Hi, yourself," she replies, her eyes opening. "Where have you been?"

"Attending to business."

"What's that supposed to mean?"

"It means we have nothing more to worry about. That situation has been dealt with."

She shakes her head.

"Every time you swear to me in riddles, it's a sure thing you've been up to something you shouldn't."

"Not the case. Scout's honor," I say crossing my heart.

Just then the front door chimes. We look at each other blankly.

"A little early for the milkman," I say.

"Maybe some Mormons here to save your soul," Bunny says.

"I'll chase them away," I say, getting to my feet. More chimes. "Impatient bastards," I mutter.

The Mormons turn out to be two LAPD detectives from the Van Nuys station. One I recognize. Butch Kramer is an old timer with grey hair and a beer belly and a mostly sunny disposition except when dealing with lowlifes. The other guy I don't know.

"Evening, Mr. Bernardi. Sorry about the hour. We've been sitting outside waiting for you to come home."

"Who'd I rob, Butch?"

"Wouldn't know, sir. All I know is, Lt. Rodriguez wants to talk to you."

"Can't it wait? I was trapped in that damned building half the day and I am really beat."

"Sorry, sir, I only do what I'm told."

Bunny appears in the doorway next to me.

"Joe, what's going on?"

"Just routine, honey. Nothing to worry about. Pete Rodriguez needs to talk to me."

"Should I call Ray?" she asks. Ray Giordano is a good friend as well as my attorney.

"No need. I should be back in less than an hour. If I'm not, call Pete."

She nods as I walk out the door and the two cops follow me to their unmarked sedan parked curbside. They didn't bother to cuff me. That's a good sign.

Pete Rodriguez is seated at his desk with nothing better to do than wait for me. He is chewing on pencil, a sure sign he is pissed which he proves when I sit down facing him.

"Where the hell have you been?" he asks rudely without the usual preliminary offer of coffee or soda.

"Out."

"Driving around without benefit of a car which I had impounded by the way? Nice trick, Joe."

"Maybe I was jogging," I suggest.

He checks a pink slip on his desk next to his phone.

"In the company of Hobart Kane who drives a '68 Pontiac LeMans, plate number VLK614? Where did all this jogging take place?"

"Will Rogers State Park," I say. "It was getting too dark for the polo ponies."

"Did you know that's your 'tell', Joe? Every time you want to lie to me or to Aaron Kleinschmidt, you jump in with a wiseacre remark instead."

"I'll try to remember that," I tell him.

"Did you shove Nathan Haller off the roof of the Universal Black Tower shortly after two o'clock this afternoon ?"

"What's that got to do with jogging?"

"Just answer the question."

"No, I did not."

"Somebody did. I hear you hated the bastard."

"And everything he stood for."

A hesitation, then Pete says, "You hated Gregory Lunsford as well."

"Where'd you get that?" I ask.

"Common knowledge." Cop talk for when a police officer doesn't want to give up a valuable informant. "Answer the question."

"I didn't care for him much, that's true."

"How much didn't you care for him, Joe?"

"What the hell is this all about, Pete?"

"Where have you been for the past two hours?"

"None of your business."

"Wrong answer."

"I told you, jogging in the moonlight, counting the stars. What's with the bug up your ass?"

Pete leans back in his chair, fixing me with a steely stare I've never seen before.

"Gregory Lunsford was shot to death in the parking level of his Westwood apartment house approximately ninety minutes ago. The doorman heard the shots and was able to grab a quick glimpse of a man running from the scene. I repeat, where have you been for the past two hours?"

CHAPTER FOURTEEN

Pete Rodriguez is a good cop and a good friend but there is no way I can answer his question. If it had been just me breaking into Nate Haller's home, I would have fessed up immediately but I am honor bound not to implicate Claudia Hicks and Bart Kane.

"I'm shocked," I say, avoiding the question, "although I suppose there are some who would say he deserved it."

"The question, Joe, and spare me any more bullshit."

I hesitate, then say, "Okay, Pete. No bullshit. I can't tell you where I was."

"Can't or won't?"

"One and the same."

"Did you kill him?" Pete asks.

"No, I didn't and you know I didn't."

"Don't be so sure about what I know. The reporters have already got the story. It'll be on the television news within the hour. The morning papers will have it on page one. This one will not go away quietly. The Chief's going to be all over Aaron and Aaron's going to be all over me and there will be an arrest within 48 hours, I guarantee it."

"Everybody covering their asses."

"Police Procedure 101. It's the opening chapter in the handbook."

"And I'm the fall guy?"

"Unless and until I can find someone better."

"You going to lock me up?"

"Thinking about it," Pete says. "I want to run it past Aaron first."

Aaron Kleinschmidt is in charge of the Homicide Bureau working out of Parker Center in downtown L.A. We go back more than twenty years when he tried to frame me for a murder I didn't commit. It didn't work and in the years that followed, Aaron got religion, abandoned the corrupt policies of the administration that had hired him and in the process he became a terrific cop and we became good friends.

"Aaron's going to bust my chops," I say.

"I know, he hates when you play Dick Tracy," Pete says, allowing himself a tiny smile, "but these are the moments he lives for."

"Do you have to tell him?"

"No."

"Then don't."

"Then where were you for the past two hours?" Pete asks again.

I hesitate for only a moment.

"Never mind. Call Aaron," I say. "Incidentally, Nate Haller didn't jump from the Tower roof. He was pushed."

"You saw it?"

"No, I got there right after it happened."

"And who was the person that you didn't see push Haller off the roof?"

"Greg Lunsford."

"The television producer?"

"That's right. I saw him duck into one of the doors leading to stairs."

"Okay, for the sake of argument," Pete says, "let's say Lunsford was on the roof."

"Right."

"That means you were on the roof, Joe. Why?"

"Haller and I had business to discuss."

"What kind of business?"

"Personal business."

"Tell me about it."

"Can't."

"You're just dying to get yourself locked up, aren't you?" Pete says.

"Not if I can help it. Let me lay something out for you and don't interrupt me."

"It'll be hard but I'll force myself."

"Years ago Lunsford and Haller were friends in Mobile, Alabama. Haller was still using his birth name, Nathan Halperin. Ditto Lunsford who was born Garry Leden in rural Georgia before he ran away from home. Haller was most likely a member of the crew of either a freighter that plied the waters of the Caribbean or he worked on one of the cruise ships based in Mobile that sailed to ports like Havana or Cancun. Lunsford was there at the same time using his real name though his friends knew him only as 'Irish'. He worked on various fishing boats out of Mobile Bay and he and Nathan Halperin were part of a group of drinking buddies that got together on a regular basis. One night a fight broke out and an out-of-town police officer was killed in the brawl. Names were taken but no one was arrested and by the next morning Garry Leden and Nathan Halperin had skipped town."

"You have proof of this?" Pete asks skeptically.

"I'm getting there. The date was February 23, 1941. The place, a waterfront dive called the Bucket of Grog. The victim, a police detective from Little Rock named John Kingsley." I go on to give him the details as they were given to me by Brett Klinger. "Twenty seven years later and the case is still open. Feel free to check it out."

"I will. " Pete says.

"Now, your turn. Have you got the security tapes from the bank lobby before and after the lockdown?"

"I've got 'em."

"They'll prove what I'm saying."

"You're not saying anything yet.

"Let's look at the tapes."

"I'll need my tech guy and he's home asleep."

"Wake him up."

"No, that would put him on double overtime. We'll wait until morning."

"Does that mean I can go home now?"

"Yes."

"Will somebody drive me?"

"No. I had your car pulled out of impound. It's parked in back."

"What time tomorrow morning?"

"Ten."

I get to my feet.

"I'll be here," I say.

"You'd better be," Pete replies.

"We need the tapes from all three cameras."

"I know."

"Just checking."

"Good night, Joe."

I head for the exit feeling a thousand eyes upon me. It's not fun being the object of suspicion in a murder case. I'm fast learning that it's not enough to be true blue, you have to appear that way as well and the officers who man the Van Nuys station seem to have their doubts.

I spend the first two or three hours in bed tossing and turning, then fall into a deep sleep and barely hear the last gasp of the alarm clock as I sit up in bed. I find a note pinned to my bathrobe.

Darling,

Supper tonight at Biff's unless you have been kept in
the slammer in which case Yvette, Bridget and I will
dine at the Cocoanut Grove. Simon and Garfunkle
tonight! Yummie! Love, Bunny

This is her not-so-subtle way of telling me I have no business playing cops and robbers at my age without suffering consequences.

Feeling abandoned and unloved, I scarf down a quick breakfast and then hop in the car for the quick trip to Van Nuys. No way do the ladies in my life enjoy Simon and Garfunkle without me along for the ride. It's two minutes past ten when I breeze into Pete Rodriguez' office. He looks at his watch, glares at me and then says,"Let's go." We trudge down to one of the interrogation rooms in the rear of the building where Pete's techie is all set up with a television set, a half dozen tapes and a VCR.

"Okay, where do we start?" the techie says when we settle in at the table.

"I need a clear full body shot of Gregory Lunsford before the alarm. Tall, longish wavy hair, three piece grey flannel suit," I say.

"Gotcha. I know the guy you mean," the techie says. "I think our best bet is Tape 2." He slips it into the VCR and the image appears on the screen. The main entrance is at the center back, people coming and going. Those coming walk directly toward the camera above them, then disappear. After about three minutes, Lunsford can be seen at the entrance. He comes in and walks directly toward the camera.

"There! Stop! Freeze it!" I say as the camera catches Lunsford in mid-stride. Strung across his middle is a gold chain. Hanging from the chain is Lunsford's gold Phi Beta Kappa key. I lean forward and point it out. "See it, Pete. The guy's cheesy Phi Beta Kappa key. Probably bought it at a five and dime." I turn to the techie. "Now I need a shot of him leaving the bank."

"Got it," the techie says, popping out the first tape and sliding in the second. It takes a moment for the image to come up and then the techie fast forwards. "It's about eleven minutes in." Faces and figures dart about, left and right, until the techie hits the Play button and the machine slows to normal speed. And here comes Lunsford. I can see him at the end of the line approaching. I wait until his full figure comes into view, then I squeeze the techie's arm. "Stop! Right there! You see it?" Lunsford's suit is rumpled. His tie is yanked down and he's sweating, all of which prove nothing. But there it is for all the world to see or perhaps more to the point, to not see. The gold chain hangs across his suit vest but the Phi Beta Key is missing.

"Gone," Pete says.

"But not forgotten. I can tell you exactly where it is. On the roof of the Black Tower at the exact spot where Lunsford struggled with Haller, where somehow the key was ripped loose and fell to the ground. That's where you'll find that key."

I look from one to the other with some satisfaction. Until now I had only been guessing. Now I've been proved right. The two men look at me, then look at each other.

"I guess it's possible," Pete says.

"Possible? It's a lead pipe cinch, Pete. What other explanation is there?"

"Yeah, like I say, possible," Pete repeats himself.

"Incidentally, Mr. Bernardi," the techie says, "obviously you were there and obviously you left but it's strange, we have no record of your doing so."

The techie has not stopped the tape and as I look at the screen, here I come, dapper and debonair in my camel's hair sport jacket, plum colored ascot and shades, all of which show, and the shaking in my shoes which does not. I put my finger to the screen again pointing myself out.

"Nice outfit," the techie says. "Your mother wouldn't know you."

"His mother wouldn't want to," Pete says snarkily. "Right after lunch I'm going up on that roof with a couple of forensic guys to see what we can find."

"I'll go with you."

"No, you won't. This is police work and you're not a cop, Joe. What you are is a certifiable pain in the ass but let's hope you're right about this one. A little prayer at this point wouldn't hurt. St. Jude's a good option. The patron saint of lost causes."

"I'll think about it," I say, knowing I won't. God and I have come to an understanding. I ignore him as best I can and when I find myself deep in a jam like the one I'm in now, I don't whine when He disappoints me. It's happened so many times, I'm used to it.

I'm not happy but I take it philosophically. Pete's right. He's the cop, I'm not and if the key is there, he'll find it. I head for home, hoping to get my alter ego, Sam August, into more trouble but when I sit down at the typewriter, I'm a blank. All I can think about is Nate Haller and Greg Lunsford and that damned dime store key. I call Bunny at her office hoping to make a lunch date. She's mired in work and brown bagging it at her desk. I try Phineas Ogilvy. He's already got a lunch date with Jerome Hellman who is planning to produce an unproduceable screenplay called 'Midnight Cowboy' based on a novel of the same name. The project has X-rated written all over it but United Artists is on board as the distributor and Dustin Hoffman has signed for one of the leads. I have been saying for years that the business is changing but this picture may be the harbinger of a full fledged revolution.

With nothing better to do I drive to Van Nuys and camp out in the waiting room of police headquarters. It's quarter past two.

My lunch has consisted of a Three Musketeers bar and two cups of black coffee. I'm ready to give up on the whole thing when Pete Rodriguez and two other guys walk through the main entrance. Pete spots me and starts toward me as his companions peel off.

"What are you doing here?" Pete asks.

"Couldn't wait for the good news," I say.

"What good news is that?" Pete asks sourly.

"You're telling me it wasn't there?"

"Not a trace and we covered the entire roof. Nice theory, Joe, but it didn't pan out."

"Lunsford was there. He pushed Haller from the roof."

"But you didn't see it, did you? In fact you can't even say for sure that Lunsford was on the roof."

"He had to be."

"I've talked to some of the television people. Lunsford was with them talking business while the lockdown was in force."

"That was after Haller was killed—"

"In fact, the only person we know for sure was on that roof was you, Joe. The injured cop and the chopper pilot both identified your photograph. Most cops would deduce that if Haller were shoved, it had been you doing the shoving."

"You think I killed him?"

"I said most cops. No, I don't think you killed him. I know you too well but a disinterested observer might conclude differently. Chief Reddin is a disinterested observer."

"Oh, now wait a minute—"

"Aaron has done this best to dissuade the Chief but he's not listening. This is a celebrity case. Sleazy tabloid publisher, well known author and screenwriter, this is not a case to be sloughed off. The press won't allow it."

"So you're saying I'm a suspect."

"No, Joe, what I'm saying is that you are THE suspect."

CHAPTER FIFTEEN

Pete doesn't arrest me. He says it's out of the kindness of his heart and that he believes in me. I say it's because he hasn't got a shred of evidence that'll stand up in court. Anyway, he lets me go and I head straight for home with Pete's admonition ringing in my ears. 'Don't leave town!' Just like Joe Friday. I'd never considered it though I could learn to love the idea if things get any worse.

As I turn onto Franklin and start toward the house, I see them from afar. A dozen or so men and women, three strange cars, a van marked station KTLA. Obviously they are waiting for me and I needn't wonder what they want. I know. But I do wonder who ratted me out and what was said. I turn into my driveway, nearly flattening a buxom babe wearing a headset and clad in a KTLA windbreaker. In front of me, Bunny's car is parked next to the garage. Good, she's home from work. My car has barely come to a stop when the ladies and gentlemen of the press are all over me like ticks on a hound dog. In the distance I can see two new strange cars approaching at breakneck speed. More minions of the press. Goody.

I am peppered with questions as I fight my way to the side door that leads into the kitchen. Any truth to the rumor that you are the man who shoved Nathan Haller off the roof of MCA's Black Tower? Is it true that you publicly threatened the man several times in the past few days? Have the police questioned you in the shooting death of Gregory Lunsford last evening? We are told you have no alibi for the time he was killed. What was the nature of your relationship to both men? My jaw is in the locked position and my gyrating arms and elbows are clearing a path. There was one last question which I really didn't hear as I stepped inside the kitchen and slammed the door.

Bunny is standing at the stove boiling water, for what purpose I do not know. She turns and hurries to me, throwing her arms around me and holding me tight. I respond in kind.

"Those people out there, they're so awful, constantly shouting and ringing the doorbell," Bunny says.

"I know," I say, "but your kind of people, cutie. You're the one that runs a newspaper."

"You know what I mean," she says defensively, jabbing an elbow into my ribs. "What is their problem?"

"Me. I'm a prime suspect in the murder of Gregory Lunsford."

"He's dead?" she asks, shocked.

"Shot to death last night in the parking garage of his apartment building in Westwood."

"And they think you did it?"

"I head the list," I say. "I'm also prominently mentioned as possibly shoving Nate Haller off the roof of the Black Tower."

"You've been busy," Bunny says.

"Not that busy," I reply. "Where are the girls?"

"Bridget's in her room recovering from the vapors. Yvette is upstairs on the phone, looking out her window, and giving her friends a blow-by-blow description of the riot in the front yard." She looks me up and down. "You know, I think you could use a beer," she says, walking to the refrigerator and retrieving a cold Coors. She pops the cap and hands it to me.

"You don't mind?" I ask.

"Why should I mind? I'm the drunk in the family, not you. I look on your infrequent beers as medicine for your mind and a sedative for your disposition."

I give her a kiss and take the beer. My Bunny has been sober for over a decade, a miracle which I attribute to three AA meetings a week and a steely resolve which refuses to give in to the allure of Jim Beam and his pals.

The phone rings. I walk over to the wall unit and pick up.

"Yeah?" I grunt.

"Yeah? Has no one yet taught you proper phone etiquette, Joseph? Yeah is beneath you."

It's my dear friend, Phineas Ogilvy, calling, no doubt, with helpful advice concerning a situation about which he knows absolutely nothing.

"Well, right now I feel like a 'yeah' kind of guy."

"As well you should. Rumors are flying around these corridors that you are the second coming of Vlad the Impaler. You need not tell me these rumors are untrue, I know they are, but how did you get yourself into this situation?"

"A long story."

"I love long stories. Tomorrow my column will deal with the tragic death of Gregory Lunsford, television schlockmeister without peer. Have you anything you would like me to say on your behalf?"

"Not really."

"Am I correct in saying that you have refused to provide an alibi for the time of Lunsford's death?'

"True enough, Phineas, and with good reason which I cannot talk about. Write your column but please, leave me out of it."

"As you wish, old top, but silence only makes your situation worse. When Lou Cioffi calls, and he will call, I suggest you play it straight with him. He won't burn you and he could help."

"I'll remember you said that."

Lou Cioffi is the top crime reporter in the city and, like Phineas, a good friend. I hope he doesn't call. I don't want to duck him and I don't want to lie to him.

"Joe!"

Bunny is calling me. I turn to her. She's looking out the front window at the gathering press.

"Aaron's here," she says.

I say a quick thanks and goodbye to Phineas and hurry to Bunny's side. My friend Aaron Kleinschmidt, chief of homicide for the LAPD, is just getting out of his Lincoln Town car. Four uniformed officers who have followed him are getting out of their squad cars and starting to move the crowd back off my property. Before Aaron has a chance to ring the doorbell, I open the door.

"Welcome, old friend. Come in out of the rabble."

I step aside for him and he sweeps by me without so much as a smile or a 'howdy do.'

"Is there something I can do for you?" I ask.

"Yes, Joe, you can tell me where you were last evening between the hours of six until nine."

"Can't do it, Aaron. Wish I could. Can't."

He turns his attention to Bunny. "Afternoon, Bunny. Can you talk some sense into this guy."

"Not often," she says.

"This guy's like a brother to me but even I can't keep him out of jail if he doesn't start to cooperate."

"Sorry. I really can't help you."

"I assume he wasn't here last night," Aaron says.

"You assume correctly, Lieutenant," Bunny says.

"Honest girl, my Bunny," I say, "No phony alibi, no lying to the cops. She'll tell you I was out for most of the day and didn't get home until one a.m. But your birddogs who were sitting on the house must have told you that already."

"Who were you with last evening, Joe?"

"I forget." Until Aaron comes up with something besides guess-work, I'll be damned if I am going to confess to breaking and entering.

"A man named Hobart Kane dropped you off here. We ran his plate. Who is he?" Aaron asks. "Come on, Joe, I know you didn't kill anybody but you're not helping yourself by remaining quiet. Who is this Kane and what were you two up to last evening?"

"Aaron, arrest me if you have to but I'm a man of my word and when I tell you and Pete Rodriguez I can't say anything, that's how it has to be."

"Would anybody like coffee?" Bunny breaks in trying to lower the tension. Aaron shakes his head. "No, thanks." I ignore her, keeping my gaze fixed on Aaron. He knows something and at the moment he's keeping it to himself. Bunny slinks back to the stove where she continues boiling the damned water.

"Do you know Andy Adams, Joe?"

"No."

"Detective Sergeant working out of West L.A. Young, smart, a Stanford graduate, got a real future. His father's a higher up with the Highway Patrol. Anyway, you know how quiet it is at the West L.A. station. Last night Andy caught two big ones. One was a break-in at Nathan Haller's house in Bel Air. The call came in a few minutes before nine. He and his partner responded. The house was empty but there was fresh debris in the fireplace. Incinerated. Still hot. Some sort of files. Paper clips and the metal in the binders survived. Know anything about that, Joe?" Aaron asks.

I shake my head. Aaron smiles. I suddenly realize I am like a little boy whose Mama has found the dirty magazines under his mattress. Aaron reaches in his pocket and takes out what appears to be a xerox copy of something. Slowly and deliberately he reaches into his suit jacket and takes out a pair of 'readers' which he puts on slowly and elaborately for effect.

"I misspoke a moment ago when I Implied that all of the file material had been incinerated. A few scraps from several pages survived because they were away from the fire. For instance, this scrap. There's not much here but this partial sentence survived. I'll read it.

```
. . . charge of shoplifting, a misdemeanor. The defendant,
Elizabeth Lesher, represented by Horace Crawford of
the county P.D. office, pleaded guilty to all charges
and paid a fine.
```

"And that's all there is." He looks over at Bunny. "Elizabeth Lesher, that is your maiden name, isn't it, Bunny.?"

"You know it is, Aaron," she says.

"Maybe I'll have that coffee, Bunny. I may be here a while," Aaron says pulling up a chair at the kitchen table. He gives me a hard look which says the time for evasion is past. Time for straight answers.

"So, Joe, tell me how your lovely wife's name became part of Nate Haller's files."

"No comment."

"Everybody knows what Haller was, a sleazy publisher and a sleazier blackmailer. And you and I know Bunny had a rough time when she was fighting the booze. I'm not here to embarrass anyone but Andy Adams is trying to solve a case and you, my friend, are front and center."

"I can't help you."

"Then maybe Hobart Kane can. He's not my friend. I don't have to worry about his sensibilities or spare his feelings. I may have to go at him with techniques we should have abandoned years ago but didn't, but I promise you, Joe, I will get to the truth."

His eyes meet mine and do not waver. Aaron has reached the limit of his civility. I don't want to contemplate what comes next.

"Let's make a deal," I say.

"What kind of a deal?" Aaron asks as Bunny slides a mug of coffee in front of him. He looks up and smiles his thanks.

"I want immunity on a charge of breaking and entering," I say. "That goes for anyone who might have been with me."

Aaron shakes his head. "You know I can't do that. I can recommend—"

"Not good enough."

"I will talk to—"

"You're still not there, Aaron."

"Okay, Joe, then I give you my word that I will twist every arm in sight to make sure you and your accomplice are not arrested, arraigned or brought to trial on that charge and if I fail, I will hand in my resignation as Chief of Detectives."

"Good enough for me, Aaron," I say.

"Joe, I said that charge. Anything to do with Haller's death, all bets are off."

"Understood. You were right. Haller had dug up some bogus stuff on Peter Falk and was threatening to publish. I knew it was meaningless garbage. I told him to stuff it which apparently wounded his masculinity which is when he produced what he had on Bunny. Arrests, jail time, all true and all part of the record. I told him I wasn't going to pay and I suppose in a roundabout way, I threatened him."

"Several times," Aaron points out.

"Maybe so and maybe I went a little over the top but I was talking about legal recourse, not physical retribution. When I saw him in the bank I started toward him and he ran for the stairs. I chased him up fourteen floors to the roof but when I got there, he was already gone, either jumped or pushed. That's when I caught a glimpse of someone I was pretty sure was Greg Lunsford leaving the roof by another stairway door. I know for a fact that Lunsford had the biggest and best motive of all for killing Haller. Ask Pete Rodriguez. He knows the whole story. Frankly, Aaron, it never occurred to me that Lunsford hadn't shoved him to his death."

"And Hobart Kane?"

"Until last year he was one of yours, Aaron. Pacific Division. He got shoved out on disability and went to work for Haller as a chauffeur-bodyguard."

"An ex-cop. That got by us," Aaron says.

"Anyway, Kane was far from a willing employee. Haller had something on him as well. Don't ask what because I don't know and I don't care, but with Haller dead, it was only a matter of time before someone started going through his belongings which included his blackmail files. I couldn't live with that and neither could Bart so we broke into his house that evening, found the material and burned it in the fireplace."

"And Kane will attest to this?"

"Given immunity, he will," I say. So far I have avoided mentioning Claudia Hicks and why should I? Nobody knows about her and she's getting one of the biggest breaks of her lifetime as a writer for Jesse Simmons' new television show. No, as far as I'm concerned she's the little girl that wasn't there.

"If true, Joe, this gets you off the hook for Gregory Lunsford's killing."

"It's true, Aaron."

"I sure as hell hope so so we can take your name off the top of the list of suspects." He gets to his feet. "Thanks again for the coffee, Bunny," he says.

"Always happy to see you, Aaron," she says.

He starts for the door.

"I'll fill in Andy Adams on everything you've told me. He's not only heading the break-in investigation, he's the lead on Lunsford's murder as well."

When we reach the door, I say to Aaron: "Incidentally I assume you know City Councilman Ted Browder."

"Sure, he's one of our biggest supporters."

"Next time you see him, tell him he has nothing to worry about," I say.

Aaron gives me a curious look.

"You mean—"

"I mean I saw his name in passing and whatever interest Haller took in the Councilman, it's now ashes, thanks to me and Bart Kane. Just another arrow in your quiver, Aaron, if you need it. Take care, buddy."

And I show him out.

CHAPTER SIXTEEN

I watch through the living room window as Aaron ducks into the back seat of the Lincoln, avoiding all invitations to comment to the press. The two squad cars remain as do the four uniformed officers and I see that something new has been added at curbside: a transportation vehicle. In the old days they called it a paddy wagon, it's chief function being to haul miscreants off to jail. I wonder if its presence here is practical or merely symbolic. The reporters are still a mass of snarling frustrated malcontents. Anything is possible.

I return to the kitchen where Bunny is dropping a half dozen eggs into her boiling water. Well, at least now I know what the water is for. Egg salad will be part of tonight's menu. I rummage through my wallet until I find the scrap of paper on which I've written a phone number. I dial it and after four rings, Bart Kane picks up. I recount my conversation with Aaron. At first he is apoplectic. To him Aaron Kleinschmidt is a high ranking by-the-book bully. I assure him that such is not the case, our names will not be revealed and we will not do a day's time for our foray into housebreaking. Not entirely convinced he hangs up with a 'We'll see' attitude.

A few seconds elapse as I pour myself a cup of coffee. The phone rings. I pick up.

"I understand you're being held prisoner in your own home by the champions of the free press." It's Lou Cioffi, crime editor for the *L.A. Times.*

"You understand completely, my friend, and I am delighted to see that you are not one of those caterwauling bloodsuckers clogging up my sidewalk."

"I value your friendship too much, Joe, to invade your space and trample your azaleas," Lou says. "Besides relaxing at my desk and tossing back two or three shooters is a lot more fun."

"For which you will be rewarded with a scoop, a gilt-edged exclusive."

"Aha, I knew there was method in my sanity. Shoot."

I recount my conversation with Aaron in detail skipping over the Haller house break-in. He listens attentively.

"So you're in the clear for the Lunsford killing," he says.

"Totally."

"I'd love to know the nature of your alibi."

"That you will never learn, my friend, so let's not waste each other's time asking."

"And if I call Aaron?"

"He'll verify that I have been exonerated, either on or off the record."

"Well, thanks for the scoop, Joe. Much appreciated," Lou says.

"What are friends for?" I ask, say goodbye and hang up. I can't wait until tomorrow morning when the clueless pencil pushers outside learn that a modicum of courtesy and common sense goes a lot farther than acting like an undisciplined bunch of backyard gossips hot on the trail of the latest dirt.

I glance out the window, startled to see one of the local anchormen halfway up my walkway being wrestled to the ground by two cops while a TV cameraman records it for posterity or at least for the 11 o'clock news. The anchorman, a shameless self-promoter, seems to be wailing something about freedom of the press. The two cops are dragging him in the direction of the paddy wagon where he will soon enjoy the freedom of a cell.

At eleven o'clock Bunny and I are in bed, she reading Fletcher Knebel's 'Vanished" while I am glued to our TV set awaiting the appearance of my favorite pompous news anchor. Finally he appears outside my house figuratively frothing at the mouth, excoriating the police and screaming coverup in my involvement in Greg Lunsford's death. When the station goes to commercial, I turn off the set and start nuzzle my bride's neck.

"What are you doing?" Bunny asks barely looking up from her book.

"Trying to start something, erotically speaking," I say.

"Quit it, Joe, I'm just at a good part."

"I have good parts, too, baby," I say, just like Bogie, as I reach under the covers and start to stroke the inside of her leg. Her eyes light up like an arcade pinball machine and the book makes it to the floor. My 44 year old queen of the prom melts into my arms and we spend twenty glorious minutes of bump and tickle after which I am spent. Bunny reaches down to the floor and retrieves her book, searching for the place where she left off. Funny I don't remember this happening when first we courted. Nonetheless I lay back on my pillow feeling immensely better than I did this morning with the weight of the world suffocating me. I may even get a decent night's sleep.

I do and the next morning I am enjoying breakfast while I read Lou Cioffi's exclusive story informing Los Angeles that I am no longer considered a suspect in the Greg Lunsford murder. Brilliantly written with a minimum of information, Lou has made me sound like an unheralded peacemaker, blood brother to Mohandas Ghandi, a victim of libelous reporting which appears in countless stories written by his borderline illiterate competitors from other venues.

The phone rings several times during breakfast. Bridget answers. Most are well wishers who knew I was innocent all the time. Some calls I duck, others I take. I chat at length with Peter Falk and Mick Clausen and avoid suck-up calls by members of the press. Then, just before nine, I get an unexpected call from Pete Rodriguez.

"You know a guy named Andy Adams?"

"Know of him. Why?"

"You do anything to piss him off?"

"Not that I know of. What's going on?"

"Got a call early this morning. He tells me to keep a close eye on you for the Haller death. Probably not an accident and probably you're involved."

"He say why?"

"He said Haller had something on you, for that garbage magazine of his."

"Not on me, on Bunny, from her drinking days when she was running around the country trying to get away from herself. I knew all about it. I laughed in his face."

A minute or two later I hang up and grab another cup of coffee. Then, at 9:06, she calls. Bertha Bowles, my partner, never one to shilly-shally, gets right to the point.

"Congratulations. I'm delighted. Now, if you are finished playing cops and robbers, we need to talk."

"Okay, Bert, talk."

"Here in my office. This morning some time."

"Sounds urgent."

"It is."

"Eleven o'clock?"

"Don't be late."

And she hangs up. Eleven o'clock. Yeah, I can handle that. I forget where I left off with Sam, either parasailing off the Oregon coast or in the arms of the gorgeous crown princess from Lichtenstein.

No matter. He'll keep. Officially I am still under scrutiny for Nat Haller's death and that is a situation which must be put to rest before I can get on with my life.

At ten to eleven I enter our offices at the Brickhouse Building to smiles, handshakes and other manifestations of congratulations. I feel as if I have just been elected mayor and with a spring in my step, I walk into Bertha's office at precisely one minute to eleven. She comes around the desk, beaming, gives me a big hug, then points to her visitor's chair. She doesn't actually say 'Sit!' but I have a queasy feeling I am not going to like this meeting.

"Okay, Bert," I say, "why am I here?"

"To discuss Peter Falk."

"Ah, one of my favorite subjects."

"I have had long and unhappy phone conversations with both NBC programming and Sid Sheinberg at Universal. What's all this about Peter refusing to do a series?"

"You knew that, Bert. I was here in the room when Peter signed the contract for the movie. We xxx'ed out the series clause and you went along with it. Peter said in no uncertain terms he had no interest in doing a series. You heard him."

"I heard him," Bert blusters. "I just didn't think he meant it."

"Well, he did and he does."

"No, Joe, this won't do. It's intolerable. You have to speak to him."

"I have spoken to him."

"Does he know how much money is involved?"

"He does."

"Maybe he's secretly the Count of Monte Cristo unlike the rest of us working stiffs," she says.

"I doubt it."

"Joe, we can't have this. It makes us look bad, as if we can't control our own client."

"Bert, if you have it in your head that you are going to be able to control Peter Falk, dismiss the notion immediately. He is his own man and marches to a drummer we have never even heard of."

She shakes her head.

"No, this cannot stand. Joe, you have to talk some sense into him."

"No."

"No?"

"No. Peter is a very bright man who knows exactly what he wants and what he doesn't want is another rat race of a series. You know, Bert, our job as managers is to consult and advise but not to dictate. I think there's something refreshing about Peter's attitude. The studios and the networks are so used to people rolling over when they throw huge amounts of money at them, they have no clue how to deal with a Peter Falk."

She frowns.

"Is it a ploy?"

"It could be but I don't think so. If the movie doesn't succeed, there will be no series. If it does succeed, he'll be in a much better position to negotiate but I believe him when he says he won't do another weekly series and no amount of money is going to overcome that."

"Insane," she mutters.

"I admire him for it," I reply, "and so would you if you gave it a second thought." I hesitate. "Are we done?"

"We're done," she says.

I come around the desk and kiss her forehead.

"You can't win 'em all, old girl. Don't fret it."

As I walk out the door, I look back and she is giving me a wan little smile. I smile back.

I walk away from her office and turn down an intersecting corridor to visit my much missed Gal Friday, Glenda Mae Brown, who for years was an invaluable collaborator in my career. As I near her door, I spot her standing there, slouched against the door jamb, holding a newspaper, a sly smile on her face. No doubt she wants to add her congratulations to those of the others.

"I can't believe you're not in jail," she says.

"What have I done now?"

"Oh, I don't know. How about making yourself at home in someone else's home when said person is not there?" She hands me the paper. "The early edition, boss. Check out Harry Frakes, page 12."

Her paper is not the Times, it is the *Herald Examiner*, L.A.s afternoon newspaper and Harry Frakes, a one-time movie critic, is now it's crime reporter. I turn to page 21 and find Frakes picture which heads his column. The picture is twenty years old when Frakes was something of a stud on the Hollywood cocktail party circuit. Today he is fat, balding and 50 but the photograph lingers on. I read the headline: LAPD PET SLIPS MURDER CHARGE.

I go to the text which basically says I have been cleared of any involvement in Greg Lunsford's death because at the time of his death, I and Bart Kane, Nate Haller's bodyguard, were busy ransacking Haller's swank Bel Air estate.

Joseph Bernardi, a special favorite of LAPD Chief of Detectives, Aaron Kleinschmidt, has admitted to breaking into Haller's home in the early evening hours after Haller fell to his death from the roof of Universal's executive building, the Black Tower. But did he? We have only Bernardi's word since no police report was filed on the alleged break-in which certainly becomes a convenient alibi regarding Lunsford's death in the parking garage of his apartment house.

So which is it, Chief Davis? Was there a break-in and if so, where's the paperwork to go with it? Note to my competitor across town: Next time you're handed something by Aaron Kleinschmidt or Joe Bernardi, Lou, check it out first and make sure you have all the facts.

I've read enough. I look into Glenda Mae's concerned face and give her an unconvincing smile as I hand her back the paper.

"See ya, babe," I say as I start off.

"Joe, where are you going?" she calls after me.

"To right a wrong," I say. "Either that or tilt at a windmill."

It doesn't take me long to drive to the offices of the Los Angeles Herald-Examiner and even less time to find the office of Harry Frakes. It's not much more than a cubbyhole and it smells of gin and sweat. In fact the whole operation reeks of desperation. The newspaper's been steadily losing readers for a decade and most experts agree, someday soon it's going to go belly up. Frakes looks up from his desk when I walk in and the fear suddenly reflected in his eyes is palpable.

"What do you want, Bernardi?" he says, subtly moving back in his chair.

"To beat the crap out of you, Harry."

"You're crazy. Get the fuck outta here."

"Sure, but first you're going to tell me the source of your column today."

I sit on the edge of his desk, staring down at him. Beads of moisture start to form on his hairless pate.

"My source is confidential," he stammers, looking for a way past me and knowing there isn't one.

"No, Harry, the information you printed is confidential which means you must have been digging around into a police report and Harry, we both know that's a big no-no. Who's your source?"

"I'm not telling you so get the hell out of here. You're not going to hurt me. You'd do a year easy on an assault charge beside which I would sue your fucking ass for every dime you've got. You hear me, big shot?"

"Oh, I hear you, Harry, believe me, but I'm not so stupid as to lay a hand on you. I'd have to be nuts. By the way, do you know

Angelo Cioffi?"

"Never heard of him."

"Lou Cioffi's little brother." I stifle a laugh. "Sorry, I just realized how idiotic that sounds. Angelo is six-two, two hundred and forty pounds or at least that's what he weighed for his last fight in Fresno. Two weeks ago. He won, by the way."

"Look, I don't know what you—"

"You know what makes Angelo such a good fighter, Harry? He's got a screw loose. Very unpredictable and sometimes very vicious. He hasn't killed anybody in the ring yet but I think it's just a matter of time."

Harry leans forward ands reaches for his phone. I slam my hand down hard on his and he yelps in pain.

"If you were planning on calling security, Harry, don't waste your time. I'm going. I just want to leave you with this warning, one friend to another. Angelo idolizes Lou and what you wrote in your column, that was a big mistake. I have no doubt that Angelo will come looking for you and he's not the gentleman I am. You'll never see him coming and when you watch him walk away you'll be lying in a heap, half-conscious, with several broken bones and bleeding like a busted fire hydrant."

"Call him off," Harry gurgles.

"I could if I wanted to, Harry. He listens to me. But I don't want to, simple as that."

"For God's sakes, Bernardi—"

"I came here with a simple request for a little information and got treated like a leper. Not smart of you, Harry. Not smart at all."

I slide off his desk and head for the door. Frakes cries out behind me.

"You want to know who slipped me the story? Okay, I'll tell you. It was the cop."

I turn back.

"Cop? What cop?" I ask.

"The cop. Adams."

"Don't screw with me, Frakes."

"Do I look like I want a few teeth knocked loose? It was Adams. Now call off the gorilla."

"I'll do my best," I say, my hand on the doorknob.

"Your best?" Frakes gasps.

"My best," I say. "Meanwhile, be careful where you go and try to have someone with you at all times, particularly at night. Angelo's a sneaky devil, as quick and as quiet as a cat. Take care, Frakes."

And then I'm out the door.

Next stop, the West Valley station and a heart to heart talk with Detective Sergeant Andy Adams, supposedly an up and coming star in the law and order pantheon. We'll see about that.

CHAPTER SEVENTEEN

It's nearly twelve-fifteen when I drive into the parking lot of the West Los Angeles Community Station on Butler Avenue. In area the West L.A. station is the largest and encompasses such diverse communities as Bel Air, Brentwood, the Palisades, Benedict Canyon and Westwood just to name a few. The Haller break-in in Bel Air and the murder of Greg Lunsford in the Westwood apartment house both fell under the jurisdiction of the West L.A. station and consequently, the purview of Detective Sergeant Andrew Adams. It is Adams I have come to see. I hope that he has a plausible explanation for what has just happened but I fear the worst. I haven't yet met Adams but I've talked to people who have. What I hear most about him is he's a smug, self-aggrandizing hot shot with his eye on the Chief's job, preferably before he turns 40.

The guy at the desk is a grey-haired three-striper named Ramirez and he tells me that Adams and a team from forensics are at the Lunsford apartment, giving it a thorough going over for possible clues. I ask Ramirez for directions and he gives me a funny look.

"I'd have thought you knew the place, Mr. Bernardi," he says.

"Well, I don't and how come you know my name?"

"Your picture was in the paper day before yesterday and, uh,-- the paper said—"

"The paper was wrong. Don't you guys read the Times? I've been cleared."

"If you say so, sir," Ramirez says, handing me a slip of paper with Lunsford's address on it.

"You mean, Adams still has me on his suspect list."

"Apartment 3G, Mr. Bernardi. I forgot to write it down."

We lock eyes. Without saying anything, he's telling me Adams is after my ass. I nod and head for the door.

Soon I'm on Wilshire Boulevard, fighting the lunchtime traffic. Westwood Boulevard looms up on my right and I head north to Weyburn where I find the late Gregory Lunsford's apartment building. It's a swank place and a far cry from the squalor of Mobile's commercial waterfront. He had come a long way but now his journey is done. I park the car and go in search of Apartment 3G.

The door is wide open and I can hear low level conversation from within. I peer into the apartment from the hallway. A fingerprint guy is dusting some of the furniture and another is going over the meager bookcase situated next to the large screen console TV. A slim young man in shirt sleeves is talking on the phone and his demeanor is animated but when he sees me, he seems to freeze in place before continuing his conversation. He looks away and a moment or two later hangs up. He turns to me and looks me up and down curiously as if examining a sideshow freak at the circus. Finally he walks toward me.

"What are you doing here, Mr. Bernardi?"

"You recognize me from my picture in the paper," I say.

"I do."

"I'm flattered, Sergeant," I reply.

"And you know me how, Mr. Bernardi?"

"Only the man in charge would dare remove his suit jacket during working hours."

"You really shouldn't be here, you know," he says.

"I wanted to talk to you about Harry Frakes and that so-called story you fed him today."

"Who says it was me?"

"He does."

"Okay. He needed a story," Adams says with a shrug, "and I needed to make a point."

"You fed him information from a confidential police report."

"No police report is confidential," he says smugly.

"Deputy Chief Kleinschmidt might disagree with that conclusion," I say.

"Kleinschmidt's a dinosaur who thinks rank has it's privileges. You claim you were breaking and entering at the Haller mansion in Bel Air when Lunsford was killed. In my book, that assertion needs paperwork to back it up. There is none. I know my manual, Mr. Bernardi. Your pal Kleinschmidt seems to have forgotten his."

I nod, looking over this self-confident prick almost with amusement.

"Tell me something, Sergeant, do you come by your rudeness naturally or did you have to learn it?"

His eyes narrow in anger followed by a humorless smile.

"I've been told you were something of a wise-ass, Bernardi. Thanks for the peek."

"It's one of my more endearing traits and I work at it. Thanks for noticing," I say pleasantly.

"Can't be helped. I have my eye on you. I wouldn't be surprised to learn that you had a pal stage that break-in and swear you were with him just so you would have an alibi when you dispatched Lunsford to Forest Lawn."

"I'm not that devious, Sergeant, but then again I never went to Stanford where they obviously teach these things."

He moves closer to me, invading my space and lowering his voice so it can't be heard by the other two men.

"Listen to me, Bernardi. You're a catch. Get it? This whole case is a career maker. Famous writer blows away successful television producer over— what? A woman? Professional jealousy? Money? Whatever it is, I'll dig it up and it'll go national and I'll be another step toward Lieutenant First Grade. For that I'll thank you as my boys drag you off in handcuffs."

"Do you really think your Daddy can protect you considering the kind of shit you're pulling and all the people you're alienating?"

"I'm doing just fine, thanks, but I appreciate your asking. You're as slick as an eel, Bernardi. No matter what kind of jams you get into, you get away with it but this is one cop who isn't going to roll over. I'm only sorry I don't have the Haller so-called suicide leap because I'm damned sure I could prove you gave the old bastard a helping hand down to the driveway."

"Lucky me then. The only cop I have to con is Pete Rodriguez."

One of Adams subordinates moves up next to him and speaks quietly in his ear.

"We're wrapped up, Sergeant."

"Good. Let's get out of here," Adams says, moving into the hallway. "Nielsen, let's go!" he shouts back into the room, then turns back to me. "Fair warning, Bernardi, I'll be watching you. Everything you do, everywhere you go. You're smart but not that smart and you're going to slip up and when you do I'll be right there."

I look past Adams as a man emerges from the elevator carrying a large brown paper wrapped item. If I had to guess I'd say dry cleaning. He comes our way.

The other forensic guy steps out into the hallway.

"Nothing, Sarge. This was pretty much a waste of time."

"Okay, let's go," Adams says as the man from the elevator reaches us.

"Lunsford?" he asks.

"What about him?" Adams says.

"I got dry cleaning here. Five dollars and seventy five cents."

"You're out of luck, sir. Mr. Lunsford is unavailable. Let's go, boys", and he starts off with his men behind him. "The super will be up in a moment, Bernardi, to lock the place up."

The dry cleaning guy shouts after him.

"Hey, what about this suit?"

"The other gentleman will take care of it," Adams calls loudly as the three of them reach the elevators.

The dry cleaning guy looks at me hopefully.

"I'm supposed to deliver this thing. I'm supposed to bring back five dollars and seventy five cents."

A thought hits me.

"Mind if I take a look?"

"Sure, why not?"

I lift up a section of brown paper and look underneath.Sure enough. Grey flannel. This is the suit that Lunsford was wearing in the bank. I am concentrating. I barely hear what the guy is saying.

"….overnight service is a buck and a half more but if you're in a hurry, we can handle it. Anyway, that's why the high price. We always deliver on time. No complaints and if we have a problem, we tell you about it. Like the cuffs, for example. Nothing we could do about them, Manny says those marks are some kind of tar that won't come out."

Now I'm dialed in.

"Tar, you say?"

"Yeah, tar like on roads or roofs. Black tar. And you can bet if Manny says it won't come out, it won't come out."

I reach for my wallet and pull out eight bucks.

"Oh, yeah, and the other thing," the guy says.

"What other thing?"

"It's in a little cellophane bag pinned to the inside pocket of the jacket."

"What thing? What are you talking about?"

"The little gold medallion with the broken clasp. It was tucked into one of the vest pockets. Also got some of that tar on it but that's not our problem. Just the suit."

I hand the guy the eight bucks and tell him to keep the change. I promise to leave the suit inside the apartment where Mr. Lunsford will see it as soon as he walks in the door. The cleaning guy, whose relationship to news outlets is non-existent, grins and thanks me and heads down the corridor to wait for the next elevator. I wait until he's gone, then take the stairs to the lobby. When I emerge I see the dry cleaning truck pulling away from the curb. With a smile on my face and a spring in my step, I make a beeline for the Bentley.

I figure it'll take me forty-five minutes to reach the Van Nuys station and I hope fervently that Pete will be there. I want it in my possession for as short a time as possible lest a befuddled press starts putting 2 and 2 together and getting 5. Usually when that happens (which it often does) I can handle them. It's when they come up with 7 that I start to sweat. Lou Cioffi is a straight shooter who knows his job, most of the others are recent college grads earning nickels and dimes and their work reflects it. Worse is the kind of instruction they are getting, even from the best journalism schools. Journalism entails the reporting of contemporary events without coloration pro or con in the narrative. More and more these days, the colleges and universities are turning out advocates and zealots who want to change the world to fit their own personal prejudices. Someone should tell them: Brenda Starr is not real. I smile when I think of Lou Cioffi and my conversation with Harry Frakes. Wouldn't it be wonderful if Lou really did have a younger brother named Angelo. It would make Lou twice as ballsy as he already is and I could borrow Angelo now and again when I needed a little physical protection.

A short time later I'm walking into the Van Nuys facility with Lunsford's newly cleaned suit slung over my shoulder. Cronin, the desk sergeant tells me Pete is out on a domestic disturbance beef in Tarzana, shots fired. I'm welcome to wait in his office. It's just past three. Do I really want to wait around for maybe an hour with my thumb up my butt waiting for Pete to return? I don't think so. On the other hand I need to get this suit properly processed by the forensic lab as soon as possible because the sooner I can prove Lunsford was up on that roof when Haller died the sooner my story will be believed.

My quandary melts away as soon as I turn and start out. Pete Rodriguez appears in the doorway coming in and spots me immediately. His attitude is one of annoyance.

"Joe, whatever you do, don't get married. Oh, I forgot, you are married." Then, quietly mimicking: "I wanna watch the ballgame. Well, I wanna watch 'All My Children'. Get your hands off that remote. Whose TV is this anyway? If you weren't so goddamned cheap we'd have two television sets, then I'd never have to look at your ugly face." Pete is still muttering under his breath as he passes me. "Come on back to the office," he says without breaking stride. I follow in his footsteps. "What's that you're carrying, your laundry?" he growls

"Not exactly."

Pete's not through griping. "Now I know why they call marriage an institution. It's like living in one. Crazy woman pulls a .38 from her apron, fires a wild shot right through the damned picture tube. Now they have no television at all. They actually have to talk to each other. He says screw that and charges out the front door. She chases after him, two more wild shots. A neighbor calls the cops and I gotta referee a screaming match between two certifiable nut cases."

He walks into his office and goes to his desk where he plops himself down in his swivel chair, still mumbling to himself. He looks up at me.

"Goddammit, Joe, I signed onto this job so I could lock up bad guys. I'm not a social worker and I'm not a marriage counselor. Next time I get a damned call like that one, I'm sending a squad car with explicit instructions. Do not return unless you have everybody in cuffs. I've had enough of this bullshit."

He stops to take a breath.

"What the hell is that you're carrying around?"

"A suit."

"Good. You could use a change of wardrobe. I'm getting tired of looking at you in those corduroy jackets with the leather elbow patches. You look like something out of Mr. Chips."

"It's not my suit, Pete. It belonged to the late Gregory Lunsford."

"And you've brought it to me why, because it's my size and needn't go to waste?"

"No, because I believe it proves that Lunsford was up on the roof when Haller was killed, a fact no one seems to want to accept but me."

I rip the brown paper away and hold the suit up for inspection.

"Take a look at the cuffs, Pete. The cleaner says those black marks were made by some kind of tar, maybe the kind of tar on the Tower roof. Also—" I fold back the jacket to reveal the inside pocket to which has been affixed a small plastic envelope carrying a small gold medallion. "Here is the missing Phi Beta Kappa key which we didn't find. The cleaner found it tucked in one of the vest pockets. If you look carefully, you'll see the clasp is broken and on the back side there are traces of that same tar."

Pete rises from his chair, his attention now fully engaged.He unpins the little plastic envelope and removes the key, then examines it carefully.

"It's my guess," I say, "that as soon as he pushed Haller over the ledge, he realized right away that the key had broken away from the gold chain. He might even have stepped on it in the struggle. Anyway he searched for the key, found it and slipped it into one of the vest pockets."

"That's a whole lot of supposing, Joe," Pete says.

"Have your lab guys compare the tar on the suit and on the medal to the tar on the Tower roof. That'll give you your answer."

"You're sure about that?" Pete asks, squinting at the key.

"I'd stake my life on it," I say.

"Or at the very least your freedom for the next twenty years," Pete says, looking up at me.

CHAPTER EIGHTEEN

I toss and turn all night. I may even have snored a bit during my fitful sessions of sleep, if any. I know all this because my rib cage has been pelted with little elbow digs, courtesy of my gorgeous wife who has departed our bed for the bathroom and her toothbrush. The clock on the night table reads 8:05.

I am understandably anxious because the police lab is diligently testing Lunsford's suit and the Phi Beta Key to determine if the tar samples match the tar on the roof of Universal's Black Tower. If so, I will be exonerated. I have high hopes that such will be the case. For a fleeting moment I consider calling Pete Rodriguez for news, if any, but decide that at this hour, such a call is more likely to piss him off more than he already is.

Bunny bounds out of the bathroom with a cheery hello and heads straight for her walk-in closet which contains more outfits than Macy's basement on a sale day. Some of them date back to the Johnson administration. Bunny is a waste not, want not kind of gal, either that or she is pathologically unable to divest herself of any garment she has ever worn at any time, even once. If all the females in the country were like Bunny, there never would have been a Good Will.

I ease out of bed and stumble to the now-vacated bathroom.

Bunny is pert and spirited when she first awakens, I am a slug. Maybe this is the secret to our happy marriage. In any case we both arrive at the breakfast table at more or less the same time and share our thoughts. She knows I'm worried and bucks me up, then proceeds to outline Yvette's comings and goings. My daughter loves me dearly but the only time she confides in me is when she has prematurely run out of allowance money. Bunny tells me that Yvette is passionately in love with a boy on the public school's chess team who takes her to movies and an occasional Friday night hop. His name is Stuart, he's short and skinny and whatever sex they've indulged in has been restricted to a good night kiss at the front door. Even then Stuart asked permission. Yvette has nothing to fear from this budding Grand Master.

At five past nine Bunny is off to her job at the Valley News and I trudge up the stairs to my office carrying my second mug of morning coffee. The idea of phoning Pete recurs and once more I suppress it. I can wait a few more hours to learn if I am to be a free man or spend the next fifteen or twenty years in San Quentin.

Bookwise, I'm in the middle of flying Sam August into a coastal town in Baja California where, using the alias Rocco Maggio, he is scheduled to meet with an infamous drug smuggler known as La Serpiente. Little does he know that his quarry is a beautiful woman who once ran a brothel in Mexico City and often slept in el presidente's bed. Not always the same presidente. I jump as the phone rings. I am deep into this passage oblivious to the outside world. Who the hell is interrupting me? More and more I am beginning to hate the telephone. I pick up.

"Who is this?" I snarl.

"Jesus, Joe, who pissed in your Wheaties this morning?"

"Who is this?" I demand, undeterred.

"Jesse Simmons and how come you misled me about this girl, this Claudia Hicks. You told me she was good."

"She is."

"You're losing your touch, Joe. She's more than good. She's terrific. I put her into script on a story notion and in four days she hands me a first class episode. Dialogue, characters, the works. It'll be first up after we air the pilot. Good? Buddy, you need your talent meter recalibrated."

"Mea culpa, Jesse. I didn't want to oversell her."

"In that you succeeded," he says with a chuckle.

After Jesse hangs up, I scrounge around my wallet for a ragged fragment of paper on which I have jotted down a phone number. I dial it. Three rings and she answers.

"I understand you are the new rising star in the Paramount lot," I say.

"Who is this?" Claudia asks warily.

"Joe Bernardi and congratulations. You've won Jesse Simmons' heart."

"Thanks, Joe, I tried real hard," she says, softening with a smile in her voice.

"I thought we'd celebrate. Let me take you to lunch." I say.

"I can handle that. Where and when.?"

"The where's a surprise. I'll pick you up at your place at twelve thirty. Give me an address."

Claudia lives in a modest apartment house in West Hollywood and she's waiting curbside when I pull up at 12:25. She's wearing a red cotton dress with a floral pattern and a white straw hat sits atop her head. If only I were twenty years younger and I'd never met Bunny— but that's a story for another day. She hops in and off we go, headed for Musso & Frank on Hollywood Boulevard, a favorite lunch rendezvous for those in the business including stars who like to be seen by adoring fans. On the way she thanks me several times for the help I have given her. Modestly I brush it off but inside I feel good about myself. I've gotten help and encouragement

176

from a lot of people along my way; it feels good to be paying back.

Bertha is sitting in a booth in the rear of the restaurant and she smiles when we approach. She puts out her hand to Claudia and they shake. Bertha points.

"Sit over there, my dear, so we can talk face to face without being bothered by my dyspeptic junior partner."

"Oh, but I find him charming," Claudia says.

"That's because you haven't known him all that long," Bertha says. A sidelong glance at me and a wink that Claudia can't see. "Now let's order drinks and luncheon and then you can tell me all about yourself."

Lunch goes well. I down two Coors and am mellow. The ladies chat at length to the point that I think Bertha has found her long lost daughter, which, of course, she never had. Finally Bertha cuts to the bottom line.

"Now Claudia," she says, "as I understand it you have no agent and no manager."

"Well, yes, that's true but I'm going to look around—"

"Look no further. Joe and I would be delighted if you would let us manage your career."

She is taken aback, looks to me and then back to Bertha.

"Oh, my gosh. I mean, sure. That would be terrific."

"We'll have to find you an agent—we don't do that sort of thing— and he or she will be top of the line. As for the rest, put yourself in our hands and I can pretty much guarantee that within two or three years you will be a power player in the television business. Can you handle that?"

"Absolutely," Claudia says.

Bertha juts out her hand. They shake. I realize I am superfluous to this conversation and drain the rest of my beer. Joe Bernardi, fairy godfather. That's me.

It's close to one-thirty when we walk outside. Bertha hands the valet her ticket. She and Claudia are going back to the office to get some papers signed and then Bertha will see that Claudia gets a ride back to her apartment. I'm parked curbside across the street so after giving my girls each a congratulatory hug, I jog to my car and head for home, only a few minutes away.

I flip on a music station which was a mistake. I'm listening to something about money by a guy named Tommy James and the Shingles, something like that, and for a guy brought up on the big bands, Tommy and his cohorts just don't cut it. Call me a fogey. I switch stations and catch the end of a news broadcast.

"Thackery, whose sister committed suicide last week, was taken into custody and is being held at Parker Center pending psychiatric evaluation at Cedars-Sinai Hospital. His sister Deanna, known professionally as Mitzi Moore, was an actress and had appeared in small parts in several episodes of Lunsford's TV shows. Lunsford, Thackery claimed, had gotten his sister pregnant and claimed he was merely doing God's work when he pumped two slugs into Lunsford as he was exiting his car three nights ago in his apartment house underground parking garage. Additional details are expected to be released tomorrow, according to a police spokesman."

Even though I have been pretty much cleared in Lunsford's death, it's comforting to know that any lingering doubts have been put to rest. One less thing to worry about. My satisfaction is short-lived. As soon as I turn onto Franklin, I sense something is wrong. My worst fears are confirmed when I see a black car parked in front of my house. Company at two in the afternoon? Unforgivable. It's only when I draw very near that I recognize the Lincoln town car that hauls Aaron Kleinschmidt from place to place. His driver, a well-muscled uniformed black officer named Cookie Willets, is leaning against the hood, contemplating my brownish parched lawn. I park in the driveway and walk back to him.

"Water shortage," I say.

"I can see that," he says.

"I hear you got Lunsford's killer."

"Seems that way," Cookie says

I nod toward the house.

"Is that why he's here, the bearer of good tidings?"

"Not sure."

"You think it could be about Nate Haller?"

"Possible."

"Did he bring his handcuffs?" I ask.

"Not that I noticed," Cookie says.

"A good sign," I say.

"If you say so," Cookie mutters laconically.

"Nice talking to you, Cookie," I say.

"Same here."

I find Aaron in the kitchen drinking tea and munching on Irish soda bread and jam courtesy of our Bridget who enjoys company of every persuasion and especially those for whom she can cook.

"The poor man got no lunch, sir. The least I could do was feed him," Bridget says.

I clap Aaron on the shoulder.

"Welcome to Bridget O'Shaughnessy's kitchen where no man ever left hungry," I say.

"And good stuff, too. A lot better than schrippen."

"Radio says you got Lunsford's killer."

"The guy's priest brought him in. Adams says he's a total fruit-cake."

"Not surprising. I take it you want to talk about Haller."

"I do."

"Let's go out back. It's a nice day."

Aaron takes his plate and his tea and we walk out to the rear patio where we sit at our cast iron umbrella table. In vain Bridget tried to force feed me a plate of my own but I fended her off, settling merely for a hot cup of Lyons Gold.

"What's the old joke?" I ask. "I have good news and I have bad news."

"Forget that, Joe," Aaron says, "I have mainly good news. First, and best of all, the crime lab was able to identify the tar scuffs on Lunsford's suit and the tar smear on the gold key as coming from the roof of the Tower."

"Wow," I say quietly. "Good for them."

"Anyway, as far as the LAPD and the District Attorney's office is concerned, you're exonerated."

"What's that mean?"

"It means they don't believe you were involved in Haller's death."

"And Greg Lunsford?"

"We can prove he was on the roof. We can't prove he was involved in Haller's death."

"You have my testimony."

"Alone and unsubstantiated, it's not enough, Joe."

"And where does that leave us, Aaron?"

"We're closing the case. In the absence of any further evidence, Haller's death will be labeled a suicide. It's over."

I stare at him in disbelief.

"It may be over for you, Aaron, but what about me? For days I've been the subject of smears and snickering. The press has me labeled as a killer. You can't just leave it that way."

"Joe, my hands are tied. We can't prove either you or Lunsford either guilty or innocent. We can't prosecute you for lack of evidence and we can't prosecute Lunsford for obvious reasons. I know you'd hoped for more but that's the best we can do. I'm sorry."

I grit my teeth feeling the anger start to well up inside of me. I've been tried in the press and found guilty and now officialdom can do nothing to help me clear my name.

"There will be a press conference at six this evening. I've been chosen to speak for the department. I will do my best for you but the bottom line is no decision. No matter how I describe it, there will be those who refuse to believe our conclusion. Some will believe Lunsford pushed him off the roof, others will look to you. It stinks but there it is".

Frustrated I stare up in the sky. I am totally screwed, now destined to carry the mark of Cain with me wherever I go. A rain-laden cloud passes in front of the sun. The sky darkens. I feel the first misty signs of drizzle. My hopes dashed, this should have been a good moment for me. Now it is the worst.

CHAPTER NINETEEN

Aaron does his best to sell the suicide angle even though there is absolutely no evidence that Nate Haller was suicidal. The press conference is covered live by station KTLA and it's apparent from the questions hurled at Aaron that skepticism abounds among the city's press corps. I have been described by my friend as an upstanding citizen of unimpeachable character. It does no good. The chopper pilot who stared me down has unhesitantly identified me. Several reporters have dug up the careless moments when I publicly berated Haller, my words more and more sounding like threats. For some queries, Aaron has only feeble responses. Nothing has changed except possibly for the worse. I continue to be totally screwed.

The following morning I make a big mistake. I turn on the bedroom television set to catch the latest news. KTLA's blowhard news-anchor-in-chief has already fitted me for prison stripes and shipped me off to Quentin for a life sentence. Aaron is accused of showing favoritism to a well-known friend and the D.A.s office of a clumsy and corrupt coverup. Bunny, who has been rummaging in her closet for today's office ensemble, emerges angrily and throws a mule at the TV set. It does no good. She hits the blowhard dead center and he continues to bloviate.

We go down to breakfast. I plan to stay in all day knowing full well that within the hour, the journalistic dregs will once again be out front with their notepads, cameras and television remotes. I have no intention of dealing with them. Today I will commune with Sam August and accept only the most important phone calls. Earlier I give Bridget a list of everyone I will speak to. It is a short list and everyone else can go to blazes. Bunny peers out the front window at one lone car, a reporter and a photographer. A temporary situation at best. She decides to git while the gittin' is good and backs out of the driveway unmolested. Bridget has returned from seeing Yvette off to school and now turns her attention to me.

"And now, sir, what would you prefer that I be preparing for the company?"

"Huh". My usual response to things domestic occurring in the household.

"The company, sir. That fine young actor and his wife, they've been invited as you well know and I need to know what to shop for."

It comes back to me. Peter Falk's wife Alyce is now in town and Bunny has asked them to dinner this evening. For a moment I consider calling the whole thing off but no, too late for that, and besides, there are things Peter and I need to discuss.

"Pot roast, rack of lamb, you decide, Bridget. You do them all so well, they will be delighted with anything you put in front of them."

"Thank you, sir, your blarney is much appreciated." she smiles. "And what time should I be serving?"

"Six-thirty sounds good to me," I say.

"And it would be if herself were to dine in the clothes she had just worn to work." She gives me a beady, disapproving look.

"Maybe seven-thirty," I correct myself.

"A wise choice," she says with a smile and bustles off to the pantry to inspect the provisions needed for tonight's meal.

Contrary to what I feared, the day proves uneventful. Aaron has dispatched one squad car and two uniforms and happily, they are enough to keep the hordes at bay and no one violates our property line. Phineas calls to commiserate, assuring me that all will be well in the end. Lou Cioffi phones to tell me that his column tomorrow will ream the LAPD from top to bottom for the way they have left me hanging unabsolved in the arena of public opinion. I ask him not to. There is nothing concrete the department can do to clear me. Better to let things gradually disappear. What Lou is planning will only exacerbate the situation. Reluctantly he agrees.

Well-wishing calls of support keep coming in and I take them gratefully but try to keep them short. Bertha is one of the first to call, offering both sympathy for my plight and total support, come what may. The words are comforting and I know she is sincere. I also know she's a pragmatist and she knows what the company is in for. In Hollywood gossip is a commodity that is not in short supply and ugly rumors do not die quietly. In the highly charged competitive world of filmmaking, it is not enough that you succeed, your best friend must also fail. Not pretty but that's how it has always been and I know that as long as a cloud of suspicion hangs over me, the firm of Bowles & Bernardi will pay a price. I know I must do something but I don't know what and so I lay it aside until some future moment when I can deal with it more clearly and rationally. Besides Sam August needs my undivided attention. I finally have him in El Serpiente's boudoir, his shirt off, and the lady making lascivious advances in his direction as a hidden camera records the encounter.

Suddenly the intercom sounds. Bunny is home, it's six-fifteen and our guests are expected momentarily. Reluctantly I throw the dust cover over my typewriter and head for the bedroom for a quick change of clothes.

Alyce Falk is a slim, attractive brunette, gamin-like, chatty and pleasant. Yvette, who now is allowed to eat with grown-up company, takes to her right away as do Bunny and I. She has the same adventurous spirit as Peter (not unusual considering they shared the Yugoslav escapade) and dinner is a big success. However I want to get Peter alone so after dessert, I suggest that he and I retreat to the patio where we can smoke a cigar without stinking up the house. Bunny readily agrees, Bridget even more so, so while the girls are in the living room gabbing about things feminine, Peter and I are lighting up in the cool evening air.

"This business with the guy going off the roof, Joe, this is very bad for you. I'm sorry. If I can help—", Peter says.

"Thanks, Pete. Can't do a thing about it until it dies a natural death."

"I remember you asking me what I knew about the guy and I said nothin' and then you saying you would handle things, not that I think this guy's nosedive had anything to do with you."

"Thanks for that, Pete. The guy had some leads on your visit to Yugoslavia and was going to make you out to be a Commie sympathizer. I straightened him out on that."

"Good thing. I would have had a go at him myself."

"So, forget Haller. Let's talk about you. I hear the picture's going well."

"Terrific. This character, Joe, he's delicious. I'm gonna hate it when the picture ends."

"There's always the series," I chide him.

"No, there isn't," he grins, taking a puff on his cigar. Not being a smoker, I've let mine go cold and now just hold it in my hand or chew on the end.

"I hear you've got a movie lined up," I say casually.

"Nothing you guys got for me. A previous commitment."

"Machine Gun McCain. Interesting title."

"Yeah."

"You think there's an Oscar-winning part in it for you?"

"What? Are you kidding? It's a dime a dozen B picture."

"Then not a big payday," I venture.

"Short money," Peter says. "I'm doing it for a friend."

"John Cassavettes," I say.

"You get around, Joe."

"I try. I admire your loyalty, Pete, but what do you think this is going to do for your career?"

"End it?" he asks with a twinkle.

"That won't happen," I say, "but it won't help."

He shrugs.

"So it won't help."

"Look, Pete, I admire your loyalty to a friend as long as you understand the package you've bought into. I nosed around, sure. This is a low budget caper film directed by a guy named Montaldo that nobody ever heard of. For lousy money you've committed to a B movie that can only hurt your career. I've talked to some of the people at Euro-International. Cassavettes is doing it only for the money so he can finance his own films. That I understand. Aside from an overabundance of loyalty, you I do not understand."

"Does this mean you want to terminate our arrangement?"

"Of course not. We don't dictate. You do what you want. We advise and you can take it or leave it."

"Well, Joe," he says, "in this case, I'm gonna leave it. I've got acquaintances in this town and I have friends and aside from you, those friends are John and Ben Gazzara and Gena Rowlands and maybe a couple of others and when a friend asks a favor, if I can, I pitch in. It's always gonna be that way so if you want to reconsider our deal, let's talk about it now."

"Nothing to reconsider, Pete. As I said, you're the boss. You call the shots and if you're convinced it's the best thing for you and your career, so be it."

"Great," he says with a grin. "I always knew you were a very smart fella."

"And I guess your attitude about no *Columbo* series, that's pretty final."

"Not pretty, Joe. Very," Peter says. "I've got an Emmy for the Dick Powell Theater. I'm proud of it but it's television. This Columbo character, I love him like he was my brother but it's television. I've got my heart set on doing films, Joe, good films with good writers and good directors and an eight or ten week shooting schedule instead of the six days they give you on a television show. Am I so crazy to want to do top notch work?"

"Like Machine Gun McCain?"

"I told you, that's a favor," Pete says.

"Television can make you a millionaire overnight."

"It can also put you into intensive care with a heart attack," he says.

"Okay, I quit," I laugh. "Have it your way, Pete. Your yacht to sail, I'm just along for the ride."

And it was at that moment that I realized that managing Peter Falk would never be easy because he is not a man who will willingly be managed. It'll be a rocky road but in the end, I'm betting a road worth traveling.

Nine-thirty rolls around and the Falks are leaving. Alyce is tired and Peter has an early call. We walk them to the front door and out to the steps. The temperature has dropped slightly but the night air is pleasant and invigorating. We say our goodbyes and they start down the walkway to the street where Peter's real car has been parked, not the beat-up Peugeot. At that moment a car pulls up and parks and Pete Rodriguez hops out from behind the wheel. He and our dinner guests nod in passing as Rodriguez moves quickly up the walk. He suddenly stops, looks back at Peter, then after a moment, continues on.

"I know that guy," Pete Rodriguez says, looking back as the

Falks drive away. "I recognize the face, maybe from a wanted poster. Can't put my finger on it."

"Abe Reles," I say. "Also known as Kid Twist. He works for Murder Incorporated."

"Come on, Joe," he says. "Murder Incorporated. That was thirty years ago, before the war." And then: "Wait a minute. That movie."

"Yeah, Pete, that movie," I say. "His name is Peter Falk, he's a new client and some day he's going to be very very famous."

"Murder Incorporated. I saw the picture and all I can say is, the guy scared the crap out of me, excuse the language, Bunny."

She smiles, then glances at me.

"No problem, Pete. I've heard worse around the house. And often."

"So, Pete," I say, "are you on duty or is this a social call."

"A little of each, Joe."

"How about a drink?" I say.

"Why not? Champagne if you've got it."

"Very funny. How about a cold beer?"

"Why not?" Pete says.

A few minutes later the three of us are seated in the living room, me and Pete with cold Coors and Bunny a glass of ginger ale.

"I have good news and I have bad news," Pete says, getting down to business.

"Wait a minute. I already played that game with Aaron."

"Fine. Now play it with me," Pete says. "First the bad news. I could have phoned but I wanted to see your face when I told you."

"This sounds serious," I say nervously.

"It is. Sergeant Andy Adams, the pride of Stanford and possessor of a thick and unsavory personnel file at headquarters, has whined and bitched once too often and a co-worker very properly ratted him out. He has been transferred, effective immediately, to the Harbor Division in San Pedro. This is a good division but much of his time will be spent dealing with teen gangs where lack of etiquette and bad manners won't be a detriment to his career. The commute from his house in Brentwood each day will be a living hell but then, he could always move close to Division headquarters. This I doubt will happen since Adams speaks not a word of Spanish and the locals don't really care for Gringos moving into their barrios."

"My heart bleeds for the guy." I say.

"Me, too," Pete replies. "I can hardly stand it."

"Now, you said something about good news?"

"Absolutely," Pete says. "There's this funny little guy, a rancher from Laramie, Wyoming—"

"This sounds like a limerick I haven't heard," I say.

"Shut up, wise guy, and listen for a change. You know the Universal Hotel?"

"Sure, it's up on the hill overlooking the studio."

"Right. Anyway, this guy from Laramie is here on vacation with his wife and he's a real shutterbug."

"Shutterbug?" Bunny says blankly.

"Amateur photographer. Always walking around with a camera hanging from their necks, shooting anything that moves. I guess if you live on a cattle ranch, L.A.'s got to seem like heaven. Anyway the guy's shooting telephoto shots of the studio, the sound stages, the back lot, when he's suddenly aware of a fight going on atop the Black Tower. He swivels his camera and starts shooting."

"You mean—?"

"Wait. Yesterday he flies home. Last night he starts developing his negatives and what do you know, Joe, there it is, clear as daylight. A close up telephoto shot of Greg Lunsford shoving Nate Haller off the Tower roof."

Every nerve in my body is alert and tingling. I shoot a look at Bunny. An anxious look has flooded her face.

"No question?"

"None. He enlarged the combatants, clearly Haller and Lunsford. I received the photo by fax an hour ago. I called him and at my request he sent copies to Aaron and also the District Attorney's office. I may be wrong but tomorrow or the next day I think you'll see that photo on the front page of the Times."

"And the Valley News," Bunny pipes up adamantly.

"Yes, ma'am, and the Valley News," Pete says with a smile.

I turn to Bunny and take her in my arms and hold her very, very tight. The nightmare is over.

THE END

AUTHOR'S NOTE

Peter Falk was something of a Renaissance man, both a talented actor and an accomplished artist, something for which he is less well known. Perhaps more than anyone else I have known, he lived by Polonius' advice to his son, Laertes. "This above all to thine own self be true." Over the course of his many years in Hollywood, he made many friends and fans as well as people who had little use for him. These were most often studio and network executives who didn't understand who he was and what he wanted, not only from his craft but his life as well. He demanded hard work and professionalism from those about him just as he demanded it of himself. He had no use for shortcuts and second bests. His motto: Do the job well or don't do it at all. After his experience with the short-lived weekly series 'The Trials of O'Brien' he was adamant about never doing a weekly series and his determination remained, even after the airing of 'Prescription:Murder' proved what every one had suspected. He was a delightful actor in a part he was born to play and the public wanted more. Peter held firm. Then in 1971 NBC came back to Universal with a proposition that would allow Falk to play Columbo in a series of 90 minute or 2 hour movies to air on Sunday night, rotating on a weekly basis with three other shows. This was more to Peter's liking and he signed up. Thus began a decade long love affair between Peter and the TV watching public. His movie career also thrived in films he would make while on hiatus, films like 'The In Laws', 'Murder by Death' and 'The Brinks Job' as well as a handful of films made with his good friends Cassavettes, Ben Gazzara, and Gena Rowlands. He even found time to star in Neil Simon's 'The Prisoner of Second Avenue' on Broadway. As for this mystery novel, the murders and the incidents surrounding them, including the two principals, Nate Haller and Gregory Lunsford, are fictional. As for the others, some are and some are not. If anyone mentioned herein feels demeaned or ill-used it was totally unintentional and I apologize here and now if such is the case. Finally, Peter's love affair with *Columbo* was not the only high spot of the year. The hush-hush Sheldon Leonard-Danny Arnold project finally came to fruition and Bill Windom snagged the starring role in a whimsical comedy called 'My World and Welcome To It'. Playing John Monroe, a Thurber-like cartoonist, Bill walked off with a much deserved Best Actor Emmy proving that good things happen to good people.

ABOUT THE AUTHOR

Peter S. Fischer is a former
television writer-producer
who currently lives in the
Monterey Bay area of Central
California. He is a co-creator
of "Murder, She Wrote" for
which he wrote over 40 scripts.
Among his other credits are
a dozen "Columbo" episodes
and a season helming "Ellery

Queen." He has also written and produced several TV mini-series
and Movies of the Week. In 1985 he was awarded an Edgar by the
Mystery Writers of America. In addition to four EMMY nomi-
nations, two Golden Globe Awards for Best TV series, and an
Anthony Award from the Boucheron, he has received the IBPA
award for the Best Mystery Novel of the Year, a Bronze Medal
from the Independent Publishers Association and an Honorable
Mention from the San Francisco Festival for his first novel.

Available at Amazon.com

www.petersfischer.com

PRAISE FOR THE HOLLYWOOD MURDER MYSTERIES

Jezebel in Blue Satin

In this stylish homage to the detective novels of Hollywood's Golden Age, a press agent stumbles across a starlet's dead body and into the seamy world of scheming players and morally bankrupt movie moguls.....An enjoyable fast-paced whodunit from opening act to final curtain.

–Kirkus Reviews

Fans of golden era Hollywood, snappy patter and Raymond Chandler will find much to like in Peter Fischer's murder mystery series, all centered on old school studio flak, Joe Bernardi, a happy-go-lucky war veteran who finds himself immersed in tough situations.....The series fills a niche that's been superseded by explosions and violence in too much of popular culture and even though jt's a world where men are men and women are dames, its glimpses at an era where the facade of glamour and sophistication hid an uglier truth are still fun to revisit.

–2012 San Francisco Book Festival, Honorable Mention

Jezebel in Blue Satin, set in 1947, finds movie studio publicist Joe Bernardi slumming it at a third rate motion picture house running on large egos and little talent. When the ingenue from the film referenced in the title winds up dead, can Joe uncover the killer before he loses his own life? Fischer makes an effortless transition from TV mystery to page turner, breathing new life into the film noir hard boiled detective tropes. Although not a professional sleuth, Joe's evolution from everyman into amateur private eye makes sense; any bad publicity can cost him his job so he has to get to the bottom of things.

–ForeWord Review

We Don't Need No Stinking Badges

A thrilling mystery packed with Hollywood glamour, intrigue and murder, set in 1948 Mexico.....Although the story features many famous faces (Humphrey Bogart, director John Huston, actor Walter Huston and novelist B. Traven, to name a few), the plot smartly focuses on those behind the scenes. The big names aren't used as gimmicks—they're merely planets for the story to rotate around. Joe Bernardi is the star of the show and this fictional tale in a real life setting (the actual set of 'Treasure of the Sierra Madre' was also fraught with problems) works well in Fischer's sure hands....A smart clever Mexican mystery.

–Kirkus Reviews

A former TV writer continues his old-time Hollywood mystery series, seamlessly interweaving fact and fiction in this drama that goes beyond the genre's cliches. "We Don't Need No Stinking Badges" again transports readers to post WWII Tinseltown inhabited by cinema publicist Joe Bernardi... Strong characterization propels this book. Toward the end the crosses and double-crosses become confusing, as seemingly inconsequential things such as a dead woman who was only mentioned in passing in the beginning now become matters on which the whole plot turns (but) such minor hiccups should not deter mystery lovers, Hollywood buffs or anyone who adores a good yarn.

–ForeWord Review

Peter S. Fischer has done it again—he has put me in a time machine and landed me in 1948. He has written a fast paced murder mystery that will have you up into the wee hours reading. If you love old movies, then this is the book for you.

–My Shelf. Com

This is a complex, well-crafted whodunit all on its own. There's plenty of action and adventure woven around the mystery and the characters are fully fashioned. The addition of the period piece of the 1940's filmmaking and the inclusion of big name stars as supporting characters is the whipped cream and cherry on top. It all comes together to make an engaging and fun read.

–Nyssa, Amazon Customer Review

Love Has Nothing to Do With It

Fischer's experience shows in 'Love Has Nothing To Do With It', an homage to film noir and the hard-boiled detective novel. The story is complicated... but Fischer never loses the thread. The story is intricate enough to be intriguing but not baffling....Joe Bernardi's swagger is authentic and entertaining. Overall he is a likable sleuth with the dogged determination to uncover the truth.... While the outcome of the murder is an unknown until the final pages of the current title, we do know that Joe Bernardi will survive at least until 1950, when further adventures await him in the forthcoming 'Everybody Wants an Oscar'.

— Clarion Review

A stylized, suspenseful Hollywood whodunit set in 1949....Goes down smooth for murder-mystery fans and Old Hollywood junkies.

— Kirkus Review

The Hollywood Murder Mysteries just might make a great Hallmark series. Let's give this book: The envelope please: FIVE GOLDEN OSCARS.

— Samfreene, Amazon Customer Review

The writing is fantastic and, for me, the topic was a true escape into our past entertainment world. Expect it to be quite different from today's! But that's why readers will enjoy visiting Hollywood as it was in the past. A marvelous concept that hopefully will continue up into the 60s and beyond. Loved it!

— GABixlerReviews

The Unkindness of Strangers

*Winner of the Benjamin Franklin Award
for Best Mystery Book of 2012
by the Independent Book Publisher's Association.*

Book One—1947
JEZEBEL IN BLUE SATIN

WWII is over and Joe Bernardi has just returned home after three years as a war correspondent in Europe. Married in the heat of passion three weeks before he shipped out, he has come home to find his wife Lydia a complete stranger. It's not long before Lydia is off to Reno for a quickie divorce which Joe won't accept. Meanwhile he's been hired as a publicist by third rate movie studio, Continental Pictures. One night he enters a darkened sound stage only to discover the dead body of ambitious, would-be actress Maggie Baumann. When the police investigate, they immediately zero in on Joe as the perp. Short on evidence they attempt to frame him and almost succeed. Who really killed Maggie? Was it the over-the-hill actress trying for a comeback? Or the talentless director with delusions of grandeur? Or maybe it was the hapless leading man whose career is headed nowhere now that the "real stars" are coming back from the war. There is no shortage of suspects as the story speeds along to its exciting and unexpected conclusion.

Book Two—1948
WE DON'T NEED NO STINKING BADGES

Joe Bernardi is the new guy in Warner Brothers' Press Department so it's no surprise when Joe is given the unenviable task of flying to Tampico, Mexico, to bail Humphrey Bogart out of jail without the world learning about it. When he arrives he discovers that Bogie isn't the problem. So-called accidents are occurring daily on the set, slowing down the filming of "The Treasure of the Sierra Madre" and putting tempers on edge. Everyone knows who's behind the sabotage. It's the local Jefe who has a finger in every illegal pie. But suddenly the intrigue widens and the murder of one of the actors throws the company into turmoil. Day by day, Joe finds himself drawn into a dangerous web of deceit, dupliciity and blackmail that nearly costs him his life.

Book Three—1949
LOVE HAS NOTHING TO DO WITH IT

Joe Bernardi's ex-wife Lydia is in big, big trouble. On a Sunday evening around midnight she is seen running from the plush offices of her one- time lover, Tyler Banks. She disappears into the night leaving Banks behind, dead on the carpet with a bullet in his head. Convinced that she is innocent, Joe enlists the help of his pal, lawyer Ray Giordano, and bail bondsman Mick Clausen, to prove Lydia's innocence, even as his assignment to publicize Jimmy Cagney's comeback movie for Warner's threatens to take up all of his time. Who really pulled the trigger that night? Was it the millionaire whose influence reached into City Hall? Or the not so grieving widow finally freed from a loveless marriage. Maybe it was the partner who wanted the business all to himself as well as the new widow. And what about the mysterious envelope, the one that disappeared and everyone claims never existed? Is it the key to the killer's identity and what is the secret that has been kept hidden for the past forty years?

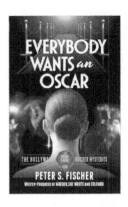

Book Four—1950
EVERYBODY WANTS AN OSCAR

After six long years Joe Bernardi's novel is at last finished and has been shipped to a publisher. But even as he awaits news, fingers crossed for luck, things are heating up at the studio. Soon production will begin on Tennessee Williams' "The Glass Menagerie" and Jane Wyman has her sights set on a second consecutive Academy Award. Jack Warner has just signed Gertrude Lawrence for the pivotal role of Amanda and is positive that the Oscar will go to Gertie. And meanwhile Eleanor Parker, who has gotten rave reviews for a prison picture called "Caged" is sure that 1950 is her year to take home the trophy. Faced with three very talented ladies all vying for his best efforts, Joe is resigned to performing a monumental juggling act. Thank God he has nothing else to worry about or at least that was the case until his agent informed him that a screenplay is floating around Hollywood that is a dead ringer for his newly completed novel. Will the ladies be forced to take a back seat as Joe goes after the thief that has stolen his work, his good name and six years of his life?

Book Five—1951
THE UNKINDNESS OF STRANGERS

Warner Brothers is getting it from all sides and Joe Bernardi seems to be everybody's favorite target. "A Streetcar Named Desire" is unproducible, they say. Too violent, too seedy, too sexy, too controversial and what's worse, it's being directed by that well-known pinko, Elia Kazan. To make matters worse, the country's number one hate monger, newspaper columnist Bryce Tremayne, is coming after Kazan with a vengeance and nothing Joe can do or say will stop him. A vicious expose column is set to run in every Hearst paper in the nation on the upcoming Sunday but a funny thing happens Friday night. Tremayne is found in a compromising condition behind the wheel of his car, a bullet hole between his eyes. Come Sunday and the scurrilous attack on Kazan does not appear. Rumors fly. Kazan is suspected but he's not the only one with a motive. Consider:

Elvira Tremayne, the unloved widow. Did Tremayne slug her one time too many?

Hubbell Cox, the flunky whose homosexuality made him a target of derision.

Willie Babbitt, the muscle. He does what he's told and what he's told to do is often unpleasant.

Jenny Coughlin, Tremayne's private secretary. But how private and what was her secret agenda?

Jed Tompkins, Elvira's father, a rich Texas cattle baron who had only contempt for his son-in-law.

Boyd Larabee, the bookkeeper, hired by Tompkins to win Cox's confidence and report back anything he's learned.

Annie Petrakis, studio makeup artist. Tremayne destroyed her lover. Has she returned the favor?

Book Six—1952
NICE GUYS FINISH DEAD

Ned Sharkey is a fugitive from mob revenge. For six years he's been successfully hiding out in the Los Angeles area while a $100, 000 contract for his demise hangs over his head. But when Warner Brothers begins filming "The Winning Team", the story of Grover Cleveland Alexander, Ned can't resist showing up at the ballpark to reunite with his old pals from the Chicago Cubs of the early 40's who have cameo roles in the film. Big mistake. When Joe Bernardi, Warner Brothers publicity guy, inadvertently sends a press release and a photo of Ned to the Chicago papers, mysterious people from the Windy City suddenly appear and a day later at break of dawn, Ned's body is found sprawled atop the pitcher's mound. It appears that someone is a hundred thousand dollars richer. Or maybe not. Who is the 22 year old kid posing as a 50 year old former hockey star? And what about Gordo Gagliano, a mountain of a man, who is out to find Ned no matter who he has to hurt to succeed? And why did baggy pants comic Fats McCoy jump Ned and try to kill him in the pool parlor? It sure wasn't about money. Joe , riddled with guilt because the photo he sent to the newspapers may have led to Ned's death, finds himself embroiled in a dangerous game of who-dun-it that leads from L. A. 's Wrigley Field to an upscale sports bar in Altadena to the posh mansions of Pasadena and finally to the swank clubhouse of Santa Anita racetrack.

Book Seven—1953
PRAY FOR US SINNERS

Joe finds himself in Quebec but it's no vacation. Alfred Hitchcock is shooting a suspenseful thriller called "I Confess" and Montgomery Clift is playing a priest accused of murder. A marriage made in heaven? Hardly. They have been at loggerheads since Day One and to make matters worse their feud is spilling out into the newspapers. When vivacious Jeanne d'Arcy, the director of the Quebec Film Commisssion volunteers to help calm the troubled waters, Joe thinks his troubles are over but that was before Jeanne got into a violent spat with a former lover and suddenly found herself under arrest on a charge of first degree murder. Guilty or not guilty? Half the clues say she did it, the other half say she is being brilliantly framed. But by who? Fingers point to the crooked Gonsalvo brothers who have ties to the Buffalo mafia family and when Joe gets too close to the truth, someone tries to shut him up. . . permanently. With the Archbishop threatening to shut down the production in the wake of the scandal, Joe finds himself torn between two loyalties.

Book Eight—1954
HAS ANYBODY HERE SEEN WYCKHAM?

Everything was going smoothly on the set of "The High and the Mighty" until the cast and crew returned from lunch. With one exception. Wiley Wyckham, the bit player sitting in seat 24A on the airliner mockup, is among the missing, and without Wyckham sitting in place, director William Wellman cannot continue filming. A studio wide search is instituted. No Wyckham. A lookalike is hired that night, filming resumes the next day and still no Wyckham. Except that by this time, it's been discovered that Wyckham, a British actor, isn't really Wyckham at all but an imposter who may very well be an agent for the Russian government, The local police call in the FBI. The FBI calls in British counterintelligence. A manhunt for the missing actor ensues and Joe Bernardi, the picture's publicist, is right in the middle of the intrigue. Everyone's upset, especially John Wayne who is furious to learn that a possible Commie spy has been working in a picture he's producing and starring in. And then they find him . It's the dead of night on the Warner Brothers backlot and Wyckham is discovered hanging by his feet from a streetlamp, his body bloodied and tortured and very much dead. and pinned to his shirt is a piece of paper with the inscription "Sic Semper Proditor". (Thus to all traitors). Who was this man who had been posing as an obscure British actor? How did he smuggle himself into the country and what has he been up to? Has he been blackmailing an important higher-up in the film business and did the victim suddenly turn on him? Is the MI6 agent from London really who he says he is and what about the reporter from the London Daily Mail who seems to know all the right questions to ask as well all the right answers.

Book Nine—1955
EYEWITNESS TO MURDER

Go to New York? Not on your life. It's a lousy idea for a movie. A two year old black and white television drama? It hasn't got a prayer. This is the age of CinemaScope and VistaVision and stereophonic sound and yes, even 3-D. Burt Lancaster and Harold Hecht must be out of their minds to think they can make a hit movie out of "Marty".
But then Joe Bernardi gets word that the love of his life, Bunny Lesher, is in New York and in trouble and so Joe changes his mind. He flies east to talk with the movie company and also to find Bunny and dig her out of whatever jam she's in. He finds that "Marty" is doing just fine but Bunny's jam is a lot bigger than he bargained for. She's being held by the police as an eyewitness to a brutal murder of a close friend in a lower Manhattan police station. Only a jammed pistol saved Bunny from being the killer's second victim and now she's in mortal danger because she knows what the man looks like and he's dead set on shutting her up. Permanently. Crooked lawyers, sleazy con artists and scheming businessmen cross Joe's path, determined to keep him from the truth and when the trail leads to the sports car racing circuit at Lime Rock in Connecticut, it's Joe who becomes the killer's prime target.

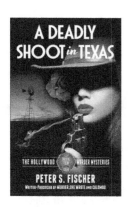

Book Ten—1956
A DEADLY SHOOT IN TEXAS

Joe Bernardi's in Marfa, Texas, and he's not happy. The tarantulas are big enough to carry off the cattle , the wind's strong enough to blow Marfa into New Mexico, and the temperature would make the Congo seem chilly. A few miles out of town Warner Brothers is shooting Edna Ferber's "Giant" with a cast that includes Rock Hudson, Elizabeth Taylor and James Dean and Jack Warner is paying through the nose for Joe's expertise as a publicist. After two days in Marfa Joe finds himself in a lonely cantina around midnight, tossing back a few cold ones, and being seduced by a gorgeous student young enough to be his daughter. The flirtation goes nowhere but the next morning little Miss Coed is found dead . And there's a problem. The coroner says she died between eight and nine o'clock. Not so fast, says Joe, who saw her alive as late as one a.m. When he points this out to the County Sheriff, all hell breaks loose and Joe becomes the target of some pretty ornery people. Like the Coroner and the Sheriff as well as the most powerful rancher in the county, his arrogant no-good son and his two flunkies, a crooked lawyer and a grieving father looking for justice or revenge, either one will do. Will Joe expose the murderer before the murderer turns Joe into Texas road kill? Tune in.

Book Eleven—1957
EVERYBODY LET'S ROCK

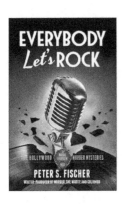

Big trouble is threatening the career of one of the country's hottest new teen idols and Joe Bernardi has been tapped to get to the bottom of it. Call it blackmail or call it extortion, a young woman claims that a nineteen year old Elvis Presley impregnated her and then helped arrange an abortion.

There's a letter and a photo to back up her claim. Nonsense, says Colonel Tom Parker, Elvis's manager and mentor. It's a damned lie. Joe is not so sure but Parker is adamant. The accusation is a totally bogus and somebody's got to prove it. But no police can be involved and no lawyers. Just a whiff of scandal and the young man's future will be destroyed, even though he's in the midst of filming a movie that could turn him into a bona fide film star. Joe heads off to Memphis under the guise of promoting Elvis's new film and finds himself mired in a web of deceit and danger. Trusted by no one he searches in vain for the woman behind the letter, crossing paths with Sam Philips of Sun Records, a vindictive alcoholic newspaper reporter, a disgraced doctor with a seedy past, and a desperate con artist determined to keep Joe from learning the truth.

Book Twelve—1958
A TOUCH OF HOMICIDE

It takes a lot to impress Joe Bernardi. He likes his job and the people he deals with but nobody is really special. Nobody, that is, except for Orson Welles, and when Avery Sterling, a bottom feeding excuse for a producer, asks Joe's help in saving Welles from an industry-wide smear campaign, Joe jumps in, heedless that the pool he has just plunged into is as dry as a vermouthless martini. A couple of days later, Sterling is found dead in his office and the police immediately zero in on two suspects—Joe who has an alibi and Welles who does not. Not to worry, there are plenty of clues at the crime scene including a blood stained monogrammed handkerchief, a rejected screenplay, a pair of black-rimmed reading glasses, a distinctive gold earring and petals from a white carnation. What's more, no less than four people threatened to kill him in front of witnesses. A case so simple a two-year old could solve it but the cop on the case is a dimwit whose uncle is on the staff of the police commissioner. Will Joe and Orson solve the case before one of them gets arrested for murder? Will an out-of-town hitman kill one or both of them? Worst of all, will Orson leave town leaving Joe holding the proverbial bag?

Book Thirteen—1959
SOME LIKE 'EM DEAD

After thirteen years, the great chase is over and Joe Bernardi is marrying Bunny Lesher. After a brief weekend honeymoon, it'll be back to work for them both; Bunny at the Valley News where she has just been named Assistant Editor and Joe publicizing Billy Wilder's new movie, Some Like It Hot about two musicians hiding out from the mob in an all-girl band. It boasts a great script and a stellar cast that includes Tony Curtis, Jack Lemmon and Marilyn Monroe, so what could go wrong? Plenty and it starts with Shirley Davenport, Bunny's protege at the News, who has been assigned to the entertainment pages. To placate Bunny and against his better judgement Joe gives Shirley a press credential for the shoot and from the start, she is a destructive force, alienating cast and crew, including Billy Wilder, who does not suffer fools easily. Someone must have become really fed up with her because one misty morning a few hundred yards down the beach from the famed Hotel Del Coronado, Shirley's lifeless body, her head bashed in with a blunt instrument, is discovered by joggers. This after she'd been seen lunching with George Raft; hobnobbing with up and coming actor, Vic Steele; angrily ignoring fellow journalist Hank Kendall; exchanging jealous looks with hair stylist Evie MacPherson; and making a general nuisance of herself everywhere she turned. United Artists is aghast and so is Joe This murder has to be solved and removed from the front pages of America's newspapers as soon as possible or when it's released, this picture will be known as 'the murder movie', hardly a selling point for a rollicking comedy.

Book Fourteen—1960
DEAD MEN PAY NO DEBTS

Among the hard and fast rules in Joe Bernardi's life is this one:
Do not, under any circumstances, travel east during the winter months. In this way one avoids dealing with snow, ice, sleet, frostbite and pneumonia. Unfortunately he has had to break this rule and having done so, is paying the price. His novel 'A Family of Strangers' has been optioned for a major motion picture and he needs to fly east in January to meet with the talented director who has taken the option. Stuart Rosenberg, in the midst of directing "Murder Inc." an expose of the 1930's gang of killers for hire, has insisted Joe write the screenplay and he needs several days to guide Joe in the right direction. Reluctantly Joe agrees, a decision which he will quickly rue when he finds himself up to his belly button with drug dealers, loan sharks, Mafia hit men, wannabe Broadway stars and an up and coming New York actor named Peter Falk who may be on the verge of stardom. Someone has beaten drug dealer Gino Finucci to death and left his body in the basement of The Mudhole, an off-off-Broadway theater which is home to Amythyst Breen, a one time darling of Broadway struggling to find her way back to the top and also Jonathan Harker, slimy and ambitious, an actor caught in the grip of drug addiction even as he struggles to get that one lucky break that will propel him to stardom. Even as Joe fights to remain above the fray, he can feel himself being inexorably drawn into the intrigue of underworld vendettas culminating in a face to face confrontation with Carlo Gambino, the boss of bosses, and the most powerful Mafia chieftain in New York City.

Book Fifteen—1961
APPLE ANNIE AND THE DUDE

Joe Bernardi is a sucker for a sad story and especially when it comes from an old pal like Lila James who, after years of trying, has landed a plum assignment as a movie publicist. Frank Capra has okayed her for his newest film, A Pocketful of Miracles, now shooting on the Paramount lot. Get this right and her little company has a big future which is when God intervenes by inflicting her with a broken leg which will put her out of commission for at least a couple of weeks. Enter Joe as Sir Galahad to save the day and fill in. A simple favor, you say? Not so fast. First he'll have to deal with Heather Leeds, Lila's assistant, an ambitious tart in the mold of Eve Harrington, a devious cupcake who makes enemies the way Betty Crocker makes biscuits. Making his job even more difficult are the on-set feuds between Bette Davis and Glenn Ford with Capra getting migraines trying to referee. And then the fun really starts as a mysterious woman named Claire Philby from Northwestern University shows up to give Heather an award and maybe something else she never bargained for. Who killed Heather Leeds? Was it Philby or maybe Heather's husband Buddy Lovejoy, a struggling television writer, or perhaps even his writing partner, Seth Donnelley. And what about Heather's ex-husband Travis Wright who was just released from prison and claims Heather owes him $9,000,000 which he left in her care? Of more concern to Joe is the shadow of suspicion that has fallen on Dexter Craven, an old friend from the Warner Bros. days. Good old Lila, she's lying peacefully in a hospital bed while Joe deals with a nest of vipers, one of which is a cold blooded killer, and a movie in the making which is being tattered by conflicting egos. It's enough to make a man long for happier days when he was slogging through muddy France at the tail-end of World War II.

Book Sixteen–1962
'TILL DEATH US DO PART

Who would want to kill a sweet old guy like Mike O'Malley, the prop master on Universal's "To Kill a Mockingbird"? Nobody, but dead he is, the victim of a hit and run that looks more like deliberate murder than accidental death. More likely the killer was after Mike's grandson Rory who had earned the enmity of Hank Greb, a burly mean-spirited teamster as well as Wayne Daniels, a wannabe actor, who claims erroneously that Rory's carelessness caused his face to be disfigured. Is this any of Joe Bernardi's business? Not really but when he showed up on the Mockingbird set as a favor to his hospitalized partner, Bertha Bowles, to woo newcomer William Windom to join the Bowles & Bernardi management firm, Joe was sucked into the situation right up to his tonsils, something he had little time for since his first priority was handling publicity for 'Lilies of the Field', a Sidney Poitier film, shooting in Tucson. Meanwhile Joe, who longs to write a second novel, has become increasingly bored with working at movie promotion and publicity. A twist of fate finds him befriended by Truman Capote and by Harper Lee who, like Joe, is trying to find that elusive second novel. Both are huge admirers of Joe's highly praised first novel and vow to help Joe get it made as a motion picture, even as Joe tries to expose the truth about Mike O'Malleys' death.

Book Seventeen—1963
CUE THE CROWS

How do you make a movie when the star of your dreams, eager to sign, is suddenly faced with a murder charge and could spend the rest of his life cooped up in San Quentin? Joe Bernardi, author, screenwriter and possibly a co-producer, has traveled north along the California coastline to Bodega Bay to hobnob with Rod Taylor who is filming Alfred Hitchcock's thriller, 'The Birds'. Rod is on the verge of signing the contract when a funny thing happens. The body of a young attractive redhead named Amanda Broome is found dead in the trunk of his Corvette. Taylor screams frame-up, even though Amanda has been stalking him for weeks and they had a violent and very public argument only hours before her body was discovered. Further filming of 'The Birds' is in jeopardy and so is the filming of Joe's movie based on his best-selling book. Looming large in the midst of this is Henrietta Boyle, a county attorney with gubernatorial ambitions and what better way to grease the path to the State House than to convict a famous movie star of homicide. But who else might have an interest in seeing Amanda dead? Perhaps her aunt, executrix of a trust fund which would have made Amanda a millionairess in a few short weeks. A definite possibility . Determined to prove Taylor innocent, Joe follows a trail that leads from a teen hangout in Palo Alto to the halls of academia to a posh country club where a triple A credit rating is the first requirement for membership. When a mysterious car tries to run Joe off the road into a deep and deadly crevasse in the hills above the Bay, he knows he's getting close to the truth but will the truth be revealed before Joe becomes buzzard bait?

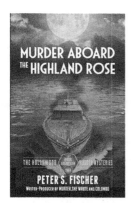

Book Eighteen—1964
MURDER ABOARD THE HIGHLAND ROSE

The night was dark. Clouds obscured the moon. The elaborate yacht owned by Joseph Kennedy lay at anchor in Monterey Bay. Shortly past midnight a shot rang out. A man aboard the yacht had been murdered. The police ferried out to the boat and found nothing amiss and the next morning Kennedy's 'Highland Rose' continued its journey north to San Francisco. Rumors abounded and for thirty-five years the events of that night in 1929 have been hidden in mystery. And now it is 1964 and it has fallen to Joe Bernardi to solve the mystery and write the book that tells the truth about that terrible night. The rumored victim, an obscure talent agent named Archie Farrell. The rumored murderer, Joseph P. Kennedy himself. Witnesses to the rumored killing, film stars Gloria Swanson and Gladys George, writer Frances Marion, and producer Edward Albee, among others. And why, after thirty-five years, has the solution to this killing become so important? Because 1964 is an election year and John F. Kennedy will be running again for the Presidency. Will he succeed? There are those who hope he will not and they are working on a hatchet job, an expose of Joe Kennedy as a philanderer and a killer showing the President to be the seed of evil. Deadly forces array themselves against Joe in his quest for truth. It appears that the secret of the Highland Rose must be kept hidden at all costs while the fate of the country hangs in the balance.

Book Nineteen—1965
ASHES TO ASHES

His name is Armitage McLeod but he is better known in the business as Anonymous Army. That's because he toils in the shadows, highly talented and well paid but none of his best movies lists his name as a screenwriter. He is a script doctor, caring little for credit. Every major studio has used him over and over again and he always delivers. He is also one of Joe Bernardi's oldest and dearest friends, a man who literally saved Joe's life on more than one occasion. And so when the phone rang in his office, Joe listened panic-stricken as Army reached out in a garbled plea for help that abruptly ended in mid-sentence. It took Joe two days to find out where Army was calling from and when he did he hopped the next available plane to Yuma, Arizona, where they were shooting a Jimmy Stewart survival picture called 'The Flight of the Phoenix'. When he arrived, he found that Army was among the missing, having disappeared without a trace throwing the production into turmoil. Despite what most directors believe, a production without a talented writer standing by for emergencies, is a production in deep trouble. Thus began a search for his old friend which suddenly threw Joe into the middle of a drug war between notorious mobster Mickey Cohen and the Crips, a bloodthirsty black gang spawned by the L.A. ghettos. His attempts to find his old friend are stymied at every turn by a bigoted chief of police and when the body of an attractive young woman is found in the desert close by the film location, Joe finds himself having to answer for a lot more than curiosity.

Book Twenty—1966
THE CASE OF THE SHAGGY STALKER

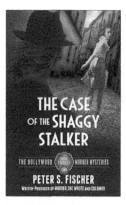

Once again there's a chance that the first Sam August film will be made because handsome and virile leading man Robert Wagner is interested. Joe Bernardi, the fertile brain behind this literary super spy, can't wait to pin Wagner down to a contract, but when he visits the set of Paul Newman's newest film, 'Harper", in which Wagner co-stars, strange circumstances pop into view. Why is Wagner's newest stand-in being introduced to him as Ben Boxer when Joe knows perfectly well that Boxer's real name is Gunnar Larsen, the number one guy in private investigator Cosmo Stryker's stable of operatives. And why can't he get straight answers to simple questions? What does Wagner need to hide? A great deal, it turns out. A schlock novelist from his wife Marian's past has turned up and is scaring the devil out of the entire family. Notifying the police is only asking for unwanted publicity, hence the services of Cosmo Stryker. But when the novelist, Horatio Cummings, is murdered in a back alley, the circumstances clumsily arranged to look like a mugging gone bad, Wagner suddenly becomes suspect number one. Luckily there exist suspects number two, three and four, etc. For example a five foot tall Cockney femme fatale and her Irish lawyer or the on-the-cheap B Movie producer Garrison King or lumbering Tough Tony Trippi, once a hero on Omaha Beach, now one of the most feared loan sharks in the city. And what's all this have to do with a woman who lays dying in a hospice in Belfast, Northern Ireland? Joe is going to have to do a lot of unraveling to get Wagner out of hot water and into his cherished movie.

Book Twenty-One—1967
WARNER'S LAST STAND

For most of us, there are times in our lives that we will remember until the day we die. Such a time occurred when Joe Bernardi received a cry for help from Jack Warner. Warner was still nominally the head of the studio but lately he had been losing his grip due to mergers and other concessions. He was personally producing Camelot with Richard Harris and Vanessa Redgrave but it was not going well. Even worse, in Texas Warren Beatty was producing and starring in something called 'Bonnie and Clyde' about a bunch of bizarre bank robbers. Part comedy and part bloody melodrama it was a movie in progress with which Warner was totally unfamiliar and he was suddenly terrified of becoming irrelevant in an industry which he had helped establish. Desperate he turned to Joe for help, begging his long time friend to travel to Texas to find out if, as he suspected, the lunatics were taking over the asylum. Never one to turn his back on an old friend, Joe traveled to Dallas where he learned first hand that Beatty was indeed creating a new kind of movie, one that threatened to change the nature of the film industry for years to come. He also found himself in the middle of a war between the authorities and the local drug lord with Joe's life and limbs squarely on the line. Beatty was not happy, rightfully aware that Joe had been asked by Warner to spy on the company. Faye Dunaway was using her considerable wiles to get Joe to create a female federal agent that Faye could ride to fame and riches in a successful film franchise while Estelle Parsons was imploring Joe to intercede on behalf of her black teamster driver who had suddenly becomes a victim of police racism. Within a couple of days Joe wished longingly that he was free of this chaos and back in Los Angeles, cuddling in the arms of his loving wife Bunny. Texas, he had discovered, was no place for the faint of heart and he had the bruises and broken ribs to prove it.

FUTURE TITLES IN THE SERIES:

Adventure Beneath the Alps

Made in the USA
Las Vegas, NV
01 May 2023

71377300R00122